BEYOND THE HOLE IN THE FENCE

GWEN BANTA

PRAISE FOR GWEN BANTA'S BEYOND THE HOLE IN THE FENCE

"A remarkable story ... I was gripped from beginning to end by this page-turner ... masterfully written." - Readers' Favorite 5 STARS (A. Boucher)

"*Beyond the Hole in the Fence* simmers with humor ... replete with twists and turns. Thoroughly absorbing from the 1st paragraph ... a rollicking ride ... an exceptionally vivid portrait of the 1950s and an atmosphere of wonder, revelation, and change." - Midwest Book Review (D. Donovan, Sr. Reviewer)

"*Beyond the Hole in the Fence* is wonderfully written with a flawless plot that flows seamlessly ... I loved the novel ... highly engaging with well-crafted dialogue that brings the story to life." - Readers' Favorite 5 STARS (F. Mutuma)

"*Beyond the Hole in the Fence* is ... a testament to the power of unconditional love and empathy ... This is excellent work, and I highly recommend this book to anyone who enjoys captivating and emotionally engaging stories." - Readers' Favorite 5 STARS (L. Nyakansaila)

ALSO BY GWEN BANTA

NOVELS

Rediscovering Ramona

The Unconventional Path of Thelonious Aubrey

Enduv Road

The Train Jumper

The Remarkable Journey of Weed Clapper

Inside Sam Lerner

With Wanton Disregard

The Fly Strip

CHILDREN'S BOOKS

The Monster Zoo

For Brian, who always found the hole in the fence.

"You don't love someone for their looks, or their clothes, or their fancy car, but because they sing a song only you can hear."

Oscar Wilde

"Life will show you masks that are worth all your carnivals."

Ralph Waldo Emerson

BOOK I: BRIGHT LIGHTS

1

HALCYON DAYS

Endicott, New York - 1950

My grandfather often said that every new day is like a bundle of Christmas. I found that to be a delightful thought once I finally reconciled his philosophy with my childhood, which could be more accurately described as a bundle of carnival freaks.

I confess that my lifestyle wasn't always so unorthodox. Although my birth name was Lorraine Merrill, everyone called me "Rainy" for short (except local delinquent Tommy DiGiovanni, who saddled me with "Drippy"). My early childhood resembled a stick drawing of a-mom-and-dad-and-dog-and-cat pastoral scene--like the kind of pictures that goofy kindergarten children create as their depiction of normalcy. But I thought I was as normal as all my other paste-eating, crayon-wielding friends ... until I had to color my parents out of my drawings.

In my memory, I keep an album of snapshots of my mom, but sometimes it's too painful to flip through the album because she died just before my eighth birthday. My mother was a gentle, soft-spoken schoolteacher who won a trip to Niagara Falls for being voted the best elementary teacher of the year in the Triple Cities, which includes Endicott, Binghamton, and Johnson City.

Dad, a baker at Eatwell Bakery, crowed with pride when we learned she had won the contest. Although he couldn't get away from work long enough to accompany her, he insisted she go see the falls. "You earned this, bunny face," he told her, "and I want you to have the time of your life. I'll take care of our puppy." (I was the puppy. My father's nicknames for people he loved revolved around soft animals with floppy ears.)

Traveling had always been my mother's dream, but two days after she arrived, she stepped backward off a cliff while taking a photo, plunging to her death onto the rocks below. The account of her fatal accident was in all the newspapers and resulted in stricter safety regulations being implemented for the area, improvements that came too late to save my mom.

My father's euphemism for her death was, "She's now resting in Niagara." He also claimed she probably passed out the second she slipped and therefore didn't suffer, which we both convinced ourselves to be true because we couldn't bear thinking of the alternative.

Not too long after my mother's accident, my dad experienced a nervous breakdown at the bakery. His only explanation was that the smell of donuts made him inexplicably sad. After an extended hospital stay, he finally returned to his job, but he took his melancholy to work with him every day for five years like a thermos of coffee in a lunch pail. There were intermittent hospital stays during those years, and with each one, I lost a bit more of my dad.

Unfortunately, the owner of the bakery eventually let him

go "for the sake of his recovery," which my grandpa declared was a cowardly way of saying; "I'm firing you because I'm a callous blockhead."

The day Dad lost his job, my irate grandpa marched over to Eatwell Bakery, pulled the boss aside, and accused the guy of being a "heartless donut-hole." (I suspect Gramps cleaned up the actual story when he related it to me.) According to Gramps, the boss sputtered like a dummy and claimed he couldn't just stand by while my dad's tears dripped all over the pastries. Gramps, with his usual touch of irony, told the boss that his muffins were tasteless anyway, so my dad was only doing him a favor. The best revenge was when Gramps spontaneously slugged an innocent-looking blueberry pie and two hapless croissants before storming out the door.

When my father lost his job permanently, I was thirteen years old. Because of my father's loss of income, we had to move out of our house on Elm Street into a roomy but modest apartment above a six-car garage on nearby Jennings Street. Gramps and my father were very close, so Grandpa gave up his flat and moved in to help us out. "You just get better," he told my dad, "I'll mind the puppy."

My grandpa, a local landscaper, would often bring home different plants and bugs to teach me about botany and entomology. He was a very funny man with mischievous blue eyes, silver hair, and a tender heart--kind of a skinny version of Santa Claus. He was my own bundle of Christmas.

Gramps was also very creative. Together, we decorated my room with paper monarch butterflies we made from newspaper and wire, and every time he would bring home a new species of caterpillar, we would create a likeness out of papier-mâché until my room looked like the Museum of Natural History. I told Gramps that all that was missing was a dinosaur, and soon afterward, a Tyrannosaurus with bloody claws showed up on my dresser.

He was also very good with chemistry, so he conducted a variety of science experiments in our kitchen like the neighborly scientist Don Herbert on the television program, "Watch Mr. Wizard." One time, Gramps caused a fizzling eruption while creating bath balls, so the ingredients oozed all over the counter like a creature from a horror movie. I loved it, of course.

Gramps knew my favorite experiments were the ones that went awry, so I always suspected that he planned the exhilarating outcome. I wasn't sure until my dad spilled the beans after Gramps botched a baking soda and vinegar experiment which caused an explosion that peeled some of the wallpaper off the kitchen wall.

"Don't let 'Mr. Wizard' fool you like he used to fool me, Rainy," my dad yelled from his bedroom, which was all the confirmation I needed that Grandpa planned his science snafus as a means of entertainment.

I know my dad and Gramps tried very hard to make my childhood seem normal, but how does a kid know what normal is, anyway? It seems to me that we define normalcy based on personal experiences, so at that point in my life, I had no concept of what was different. And yet my childhood turned out to be as unconventional as one might ever imagine.

————

As time passed, Dad's doctors prescribed a variety of medications for him, but he continued to slip deeper into depression; and every week he became thinner and weaker. Grandpa and I did the cooking and cleaning while my father stayed in bed most of the time.

Grandpa's cooking was very creative. He made grilled cheese with pickles, and beans on toast with shaved carrots on top. (The carrots were to ensure that I met the USDA's recommended daily quota of vegetables in case the Endicott Nutrition S.S. ever knocked on our door to inquire.)

Although we had limited funds, Gramps always made dinner fun. Each week, he brought home a gooey jelly roll from the A&P Grocery. I always got the biggest slice of the pinwheel-like confection. To make it as "Parisian as the Eiffel Tower," Grandpa added a dollop of his homemade strawberry jam on top, undaunted by the threat of cavities.

My father stopped coming to the dinner table, so we served him his meals in bed. Gramps tried to make him laugh by playing pranks in hopes the silliness would lift Dad's spirits. One day, he bought home plastic ice cubes that contained bug-eyed insects and served them to my father in a glass of lemonade. Dad didn't laugh much anymore, so when he feigned horror, we were delighted.

On another occasion, Gramps, pretending to discover something "nasally offensive" on his shoe, scraped it off and then licked his finger to identify the brown substance. "Yup," he said, "it's that tick-riddled dog with the overactive bowels that belongs to the Westons."

On his cue, I scooped up a finger-full to taste for myself. "Hmm ... I think you're right, Gramps. That's beagle poop."

Of course, it was peanut butter, but Dad laughed loudly anyway. We were encouraged each time he laughed, although even then, I knew those moments were rapidly slipping away.

2

HONKY-TONK

On evenings when my dad was sleeping, my grandfather often took me with him to Jukie's, a local music hall on Nanticoke Avenue. The music hall exposed me to folks who were different from the people in my neighborhood and school. Our evenings at Jukie's helped me see color in the world during a time when my days were becoming increasingly gray.

We had to walk about eight blocks to the music hall, which was over a rundown sundry store on one of the more seedy blocks beyond our neighborhood. Occasionally, a shifty character eyed us as we passed by, so Grandpa always insisted on taking my hand, despite my protests that I was too old for hand-holding.

"Gramps, I'm nearly fourteen, so you don't need to protect me. I appreciate your concern, but I'm not going to fall down a cliff," I protested, "so how 'bout if we just agree that you can hold my hand if we ever visit Niagara Falls? Whaddya say? (Negotiation was one of my favorite tactics.)

"If we ever go to those damn falls, I'll strap an inflatable raft and a parachute on your back and make you wear a buoy on your head, Lorraine Merrill!"

"But what if someone sees you holding my hand like a little kid? I'll get bullied at school. I think we stand out too much, Gramps."

"That's exactly my concern. So hold on, or next time we come, you'll stand out even more because I'll make you wear a hat with a chicken on top."

"I'm pretty sure you don't have a chicken hat.

"No, but I know where to get a chicken." He clucked loudly, which made me laugh despite my embarrassment.

I was always full of anticipation as we approached the dance hall. Although I felt guilty about leaving my father home alone, I knew there would be laughter, music, shouting, singing, and maybe even a fight or two, which was the pièce de résistance of eye-popping entertainment.

By the time we arrived, my stomach was like a sack of Mexican jumping beans. There were two stairways to the upstairs dance hall. One was an outdoor stairway that patrons had to access by walking around the building, and the other was a cozy, curved staircase right inside the entry, offering quick relief from the cold.

"Gramps, please let's get inside fast where it's warm."

"Honey, you know we always use the outside stairway that the Negro folks use."

"But we're not Negroes."

"We're not?"

"I think I would have noticed if we were."

"Color is just a concept, my dear. I learned that lesson in the war. In a foxhole, you find out real fast that everybody's blood is the same color. And white folks shouldn't have more privileges than our friends."

"I understand, but it only makes sense that everyone

should use the inside stairway where it's warm and less slippery. That would be safer for everybody."

"You know the rule—they're restricted."

"Yes, I know--because of their color, but that's really stupid!"

"It certainly is, but to some folks who live black-and-white lives, color is a negative thing. Always remember that the quality of your life is determined by the colors in your spectrum."

As we started up the wooden staircase behind the brick building, I could hear the music pulsating from inside the room. The warm lights were shining through the window, and as always, I was filled with anticipation.

"I hear da beat, so let's move dem feets." That was Grandpa's corny line each time we reached the top of the staircase. As we opened the door, there was an explosion of energy as the promise of adventure beckoned us in.

The dance hall was not fancy, but it felt rich with its varnished wood floors and rose-tinted walls. Warm lighting saturated the room in tones that smiled in greeting. The big glass ball that hung in the middle of the ceiling was covered with pieces of mirror that reflected the festive colors of the garments worn by all the women patrons as they sashayed around the dance hall.

Although the room did not have a bar, the patrons continually passed around thermos bottles full of liquor like a fire bucket brigade. Grandpa described nights at Jukie's as an "86.5 proof progressive dinner."

Every evening, the activity paused long enough for an officiant, who usually was Gramps, to extract a numbered ball out of a spinning cage before our friend Primrose called out the number to the roomful of rapt listeners. Then someone in the crowd would hoot and cheer when they won the money in the lottery bowl. And almost always, the winner would slip a few coins into my hand so I would feel like a winner too.

Primrose was my image of a goddess with her burnished-brown skin and Chicklet-white teeth. She was tall, with a plump midline, wide shoulders, and an ample bosom to support a laugh that reverberated like the engine of an old Ford truck. When Primrose hugged me, I felt so safe that I wanted to bury my head in her chest to breathe in her intoxicating scent, which was a mixture of rum and lilacs.

Gramps played everything from standards to boogie-woogie to honky-tonk, and Prim loved to sing along with the music. Her dulcet voice was like warm apple pie and as satisfying as her hugs. Grandpa would often draw out a song as long as possible just so Primrose would keep singing. She could sing anything, but my favorite tune was her version of the Etta James hit, "Roll With Me Henry," which always got the place rocking till the light fixtures shook.

I was old enough to notice that Primrose had a big crush on Gramps. When I asked him about her one night during a break in the music, he whispered, "She sure is a fine lady, but it wouldn't be appropriate for me to take her out in public. Mixed couples can run into trouble, and I would never put her in that situation. But let's have her over for dinner sometime. What do you say to that, kiddo?"

"Can she do the cooking?" I teased.

"What? Nothing can top my tuna volcano. You have no sense of adventure, Rainy!" he laughed. "Break is over. They're calling for us to keep the party going. What would you like to hear next?"

"'Heart of My Heart'!" I answered without hesitation, knowing it was a crowd favorite. We carried on with gusto until it was time to close up and go home. After the last song, everyone stood up and pledged allegiance to the flag while

Grandpa played the "Star-Spangled Banner," which was one of my favorite moments of every visit. We all placed our hands on our hearts as we proudly demonstrated our patriotism.

After the dance hall closed, we usually hitched a ride home with old John Joe, who wore bead necklaces and a feather in his hat. He was always happy to let us squeeze into the cab of his beloved Chevy truck he had dubbed "Pocahontas." He talked to her as if she were human, and sometimes he paused for her to answer while Gramps and I waited patiently for signs of life. Finally, John Joe would nod as if answering, and then he would start her up so we could all head home.

John Joe, who claimed to be a descendant of Chief Crazy Horse, was very outgoing but a little whacky. One evening, Gramps told him he was more accurately a descendant of "Chief Crazy Horse's Ass," which made me laugh so hard that I peed on the seat. I was horrified, but John Joe assured me that it was an honor that it was I who had baptized his truck and that now he would be safe in his Chevy forever.

As usual, that night at Jukie's was a wonderful escape, although I had no way of knowing it would be my last evening to ever visit the dance hall with Gramps. I truly believed that my life was looking up, but I had yet to learn that even when looking, we can't truly see what is in front of us.

3

CARNIVAL

It was June 1951. Our school term was over, and the excitement of summer vacation had set in. I loved it when summer rolled around, not only because Endicott was too cold in the winter, but also because summer was the season when the nearby woods came alive with violets and Lilies of the Valley, caterpillars, butterflies, and lightning bugs.

Neighborhood friends of all ages usually hung out in the woods at the end of Elm Street behind Frey Avenue, where we picked wildflowers, climbed trees, and raced the cottontail rabbits through the tall grass to test our speed. Our favorite gathering spot was the creek that meandered lazily through the woods. The younger kids collected turtles for pets while the teenagers competed by catching minnows in our hands to improve reflexes as we revved up for street softball.

In one area of the creek, the water was deep enough to swim. Somewhere in the past, a clever local had mounted a rope on a sturdy branch of a maple tree and then nailed horizontal footholds up one side of its trunk so swimmers could climb to the top, grab the rope, and swing far out over the water.

There was a certain protocol for using the rope swing. Although there were constant fights in the neighborhood, no one tried to jump the line to the rope swing. It was forbidden. The older swimmers would grab the rope for the younger children and bring it close to shore so that those who were deemed too small to climb the tree (by democratic process, of course) could take flight from the edge of the creek bed. They would also stay vigilant to make sure no little heads went underwater without popping up again.

Endicott, home of E-J Shoes, was a company town where even the most self-absorbed teenagers in the neighborhood were ingrained with a collective sense of responsibility and an "all-for-one" attitude (exemplified by regular group efforts to sneak each other through the back door of the Starlight Movie Theater.)

While frolicking at the creek, the worst injury was usually an ear infection, although my friend Margie White once fell out of a tree and broke her tailbone. After immediately forming an ad hoc group of paramedics, Tommy DiGiovanni, Rene Hardy and I placed Margie on an old log and dragged her up Maple Street until we got her safely home. It was a group effort, and we felt like Purple Heart-worthy heroes. (Margie, who winced every time the log hit a crack in the sidewalk, undoubtedly viewed the whole painful event in a different light.)

The greatest highlight of the summer was the arrival of the carnival. Once a year, the carnival pulled into town, and the workers would begin to set up without fanfare on the hill above the creek where we played. Word-of-mouth among us carnival enthusiasts was like a slow and steady heartbeat. The air of anticipation started as soon as we saw tent poles going up and the fencing being positioned around the grounds. Every day, we walked to the creek to watch the progress. When the carnies began stringing the lights, the excitement would heighten exponentially.

Once the tents were erected, groups of local kids climbed the wooded hill above the creek and peered through the fencing to watch the buzz of activity inside. Some of the workers were quite strange, but they were always friendly. Often they would wave and invite us all to come join them as soon as they opened for business.

The summer was hot and humid, but the carnies worked rapidly, and despite the heat, they appeared to enjoy their work. There was frequent shouting and laughter from inside the grounds, and a crescendo of raucous cheers every time a tent was finally brought to a standing position.

The carnies usually kept to themselves. However, when a few workers slipped down the hill for a dip in the creek to cool off one scorching evening, someone local complained and called the police.

I must admit that the police chase was thrilling. We raced out onto the streets to see what the commotion was and followed the police cars down to the woods. The police drilled their spotlights into the backs of the escaping carnies as they scrambled back up the hillside to their encampment or hid behind trees to camouflage themselves.

Everyone who had gathered cheered the chase, although I'm not sure for whom we were rooting. We simply fed off the excitement of it all, blind to the injustice and prejudice of the entire event.

I didn't understand at the time why anyone would be forbidden to cool off in a public creek. After all, I knew darn well that Rusty Smith peed in the water all the time. He even bragged about it, and no one chased him out of the water. I quickly discovered that carnies were just as unacceptable as people like Primrose. But Prim was a different color, whereas many carnival employees were white, so the whole event was confounding.

When I asked my grandfather why the carnival employees were not permitted to swim in the creek, he explained that the carnies were only allowed in town if they stayed with "their kind." (He said it with quote fingers.) "They are eccentric, Rainy, and that scares some folks. People make up lies about those who are unique."

"What lies?"

"There are all sorts of rumors that carnies are gypsies who kidnap white children, hypnotize them, and then dye their skin with walnut stain so they can never be identified. I'm not sure who comes up with such preposterous theories, but I believe such fear-mongering is advanced by bad people who harbor dark thoughts about anyone who is different."

"I'm still confused. If there isn't an actual law that carnies can't swim in the creek, how can the cops get away with chasing them out? Do they also think they're bad seeds like some of the parents say?"

"Perhaps ... and there may actually be a few undesirables in the carnival, maybe even some ex-convicts, but we have one of those here in our own neighborhood. I bet you didn't know that old man Hardy was arrested once for stealing someone's car, and yet he's one of the first people to judge others."

"He's disgusting."

"Yes, but I've learned that it's part of the human condition to look down upon someone else as a means of elevating one's self-esteem. You must always remember to offer a hand up rather than a look down, child."

I didn't quite understand what he meant, but it would only be a short while before I would learn.

———

The arrival of the carnival filled all the children with an industrious spirit. Being a neighborhood of limited wealth, the younger inhabitants had to find creative means to make "throwaway money," which was the adults' assessment of money spent foolishly on sweets and amusement rides.

Therefore, each summer, those of us who counted the days leading up to the opening of the carnival went door-to-door offering to mow lawns, wash windows, weed flowerbeds, wax cars, babysit, run errands, and clean garages. However, the parents were of limited means also, so there wasn't too much extra cash to go around.

It was the teenagers who usually generated the most income because they could provide more advanced services than the woeful youth. However, the younger kids who were determined enough to join the troops of door-knocking teenagers sold homemade potholders and greeting cards (happily purchased out of pity for the pathetic efforts of the little goofballs), or soup cans of recently unearthed fishing worms (begrudgingly purchased by neighbors who had never held a fishing rod but were desperate to avoid a lawn covered with abandoned crawlers.)

That summer, my last summer in Endicott, I started a storytelling hour in the yard next to our garage apartment and charged each of the neighborhood children a nickel to attend. The mothers happily paid because that gave them a break every afternoon. My stories were quite inventive, so my storytelling hour was an unexpected success, and I earned enough money to buy tickets for me and Gramps to go to the carnival.

By then, Daddy was sleeping all the time, and he looked even older than my grandpa. He had been in bed so long that he could no longer walk very far, so I didn't offer a ticket to him. I didn't want him to feel bad that he couldn't participate, but at that point, I don't think he even understood much of what I said anymore. He mumbled a lot, and I always felt as if he were saying a slow goodbye.

On the night Grandpa and I decided to go to the carnival, Grandpa gently covered my dad with blankets. That was odd to me because it was a blistering hot summer evening, but I knew it was my grandfather's way of telling his son he loved him.

"Your dad would want you to have a wonderful time tonight, Rainy," Gramps told me after he closed Dad's bedroom door. "He's all tucked in safely, so how about if we ditch this place and go take in the colors of the night?"

4

THE LIGHTS ON THE HILL

The night was sweltering. I had on a pair of shorts and a sleeveless cotton shirt, and I gathered my hair off my neck into a ponytail. Grandpa said he would've worn shorts too, but he was afraid his legs would drive all the women wild.

We didn't have a car to drive to the carnival, so I suggested that rather than walk all the way around the hill to the front gate on Main Street, we wade through the creek. Gramps acquiesced because he knew I loved to trounce through the cool water.

With only the illumination of a flashlight, we then climbed the hillside in the dark before entering the show through a loading gate in the back. It felt more special that way-like the carnival belonged only to us and our neighborhood.

From the moment of our arrival, the carnival was an onslaught of stimulation. The music was very loud, and the lights were even louder. Even the giant Ferris wheel, the Flying Swings, and the Tilt-A-Whirl in the bustling amusement area seemed to move to the same rhythm. Carnival workers called out to us every time we walked past a booth, urging us to shoot water guns at plastic ducks or land coins on dishes. We were urged to guess someone's weight for a prize of a kewpie doll, a stuffed animal, or an unsuspecting goldfish. We didn't have extra money to play, but we enjoyed speaking to the carnies and watching enthusiastic young men trying to win a prize for their sweethearts.

Grandpa made me keep walking as we came close to the Great Oddities tent, even though I wanted to linger to look at some of the enlarged images on the tent wall. The carnival flyers claimed to have the fattest person alive, the world's skinniest person, people with no legs, and physical oddities known as pinheads. There was one woman who was "half man," a bearded lady, and a man who was a giant.

The carnival offered everything short of President Truman on a unicycle. I was repulsed, fascinated, and excited all at the same time. Although I was sure I could sneak into the back of the Great Oddities tent if I were with Tommy, with Gramps, I'd be courting disaster.

When we got to the Ferris wheel, Gramps insisted on buying me a ticket to ride. I was thrilled. The wheel at our carnival was very tall—so tall I could look down on much of Endicott and even into our neighborhood. The lights were dazzling, and the Parisian music was loud and cheerful. I was flying freely, and everything was right in my world. There was no dead mom and no sick father. There was only warm air and lightness. Each time we went around, I waved to Gramps, who had a huge smile on his face, but I was sure my grin was even bigger.

After the ride ended, I felt lighter. It was almost impossible to walk without a spring in my step. Grandpa had enough money with him to buy us corn dogs and one cup of icy lemonade, which we shared. We slathered ketchup atop the corn dogs and chewed them as we walked along. I took small bites because I wanted to make mine last as long as possible.

There was a lot of excitement at the end of the amusement area where a crowd was gathered around another large tent that had an open stage in front of it. When we arrived, a spirited showman was stirring the crowd with promises of "titillating" excitement. Although I didn't know what titillating meant, I figured it out pretty quickly when half-clad women came out on the stage and slithered about with slow, suggestive gyrations.

The ladies were very graceful, so their moves were beautiful and tawdry all at the same time. There was also something playful and humorous in their attitudes as they winked and waved at folks in the crowd.

"I think we should keep moving," Grandpa said to me. "This is a burlesque show, which is more appropriate for adults, kiddo."

"Why, Grandpa? The ladies have clothes on, and they're using big fans to cover themselves. They don't behave any worse than Margie White does in that new bathing suit of hers whenever boys are around."

"Well, their parts are a bit more developed than Margie's. There's a lot more shaking and flopping going on up there. Margie couldn't create waves like that if she hopped around on a pogo stick."

"I'm sure she'll try that next," I laughed. "But do you think this kind of dancing is inappropriate?"

"No, do you? I think 'expressive' is a better word. The ladies don't completely undress, at least not in this carnival that comes here every year. It's mostly family-oriented, but they like to put on a show. The dancers can inspire the imagination, which makes them 'artists,' one might say. And I am one person who would say that."

"I always learn a lot from you, Gramps. You have a great perspective on everything."

"Perspective is always based on what shoes you're standing in, Rainy. All I know is that times are tough, and those ladies up there are just making a living as best they can."

"Would you go inside the tent to watch if you didn't have me with you?"

"I never have, but I wouldn't ever say no. I enjoy the music, and I like the fact that the show is egalitarian. The dancers are of different races, which no doubt makes the show even more scandalous and lurid to some people. But I'm never one to shy away from a scandal when there are democratic principles involved," he added with a wink.

"Everyone else seems to be enjoying it too. The entire crowd is moving and clapping to the music."

"That chap is a good pianist." Gramps nodded to the young man who was playing a piano that was set up outside the tent. "I could listen to him play all day. Life is music. There is music for every feeling and every event in life. It is a universal language, and each note is a word."

"I think I know what you mean, Gramps."

"What is the music saying to you?"

"I'm not quite sure, but it fills me with a sense of expectancy."

"Like a bundle of Christmas?"

"Exactly ... like something extraordinary is about to happen."

I didn't know it then, but my prediction was so accurate that a turban was all I needed to ensure my future as a fortune teller.

5

NIGHT MANEUVERS

The description most commonly used regarding Tommy DiGiovanni was "impossibly incorrigible." To me, he was just the right amount of incorrigible. He had no supervision at home and therefore, he had become a night marauder. After dark, I would look out of my bedroom window and see him standing under a street lamp smoking a cigarette. He was my age, but he seemed much older and more sophisticated. Sometimes he would see me in the light through the window and wave. I think he was more bored than anything else and just looking for something to do.

One day when we were swimming in the creek, he confessed to me that after curfew, he would sneak out of the house and go to the carnival every night it was in town. "Where do you get the money to go to the carnival every night?" I queried, knowing his family was as hard-pressed for cash as mine was.

"You sure are naïve, Rainy. No one pays. The fence is not tight to the ground, so some of us guys just sneak in under the fence. I've been doing it since I was eight. One person holds up the chain link fence while the other person crawls under. It's super easy, and we never get caught. Why don't you sneak out with me tonight and I'll show you how it's done? It's easier with two people."

I can't claim to be innocent of nighttime hijinks, because I had sneaked out at night a few times before when I wanted to catch lightning bugs. Grandpa always waited for me to fall asleep before he would allow himself to go to bed, and each night he checked in on me. But I had mastered an excellent snoring sound that was soft, low, and quite convincing. I considered myself to be the Sarah Bernhardt of snoring.

Sneaking out was easy because I didn't have to go out the front door and down the wooden stairs, an escape route that made way too much noise. It was my good luck that there was a wrought iron trellis along the side of the house. The landlord had placed it there to grow morning glories but had finally given up on the idea. No doubt my footsteps on the trellis had added to the demise of the vines, so I apologized to the flowers every time I trounced up and down the trellis. I don't suppose that helped the vines, but it assuaged my flower-assassin guilt.

I was so enamored of the carnival that I agreed to meet Tommy the night after Grandpa and I attended. Admittedly, I was terrified about our entire plan, but the fact that we were sneaking out only heightened the anticipation.

Even though I could see Tommy pacing out by the street-light, I waited an appropriate amount of time after Grandpa turned off the light before I scaled down the trellis to meet my cohort in crime.

We ran the distance to the creek, where we took off our shoes to wade across, just as Gramps and I had done the night before. After slipping back into our shoes, we scaled what Tommy dramatically called the "escarpment of escape" to the glaring lights that greeted us like a beacon in the night.

An expert at subterfuge, Tommy knew exactly which section of the fence would allow us access. Per his instructions, we followed the fence line to three large rocks in the field. He explained how the carny workers could never tighten the fence securely near the bottom of the rocks, allowing "budget-minded kids" to sneak in unnoticed through the hole at the bottom.

He was right. Once we found the rocks, we crept under the wire fence on our elbows like soldiers, and I proved to be quite proficient at belly-crawling. Within seconds, we were inside, and my heart raced with the thrill and triumph of unlawful entrance.

Immediately, we headed toward the amusements, and I was wide-eyed with excitement. Tommy had some extra change and bought a large cotton candy for us to share. While sucking on the spun sugar, I had to suppress my urge to let out a large whoop. The coloring in the sugar discolored our faces and fingers, so under the carnival lights, we looked like neon flamingos.

As we scarfed down our cotton candy, we stopped to watch the Tilt-A-Whirl go around. "Hey Melba," Tommy called to the tall and shockingly thin woman who was running the ride. I had never seen a person so skinny. She was a stick figure, with pale skin so painfully stretched across her bony skeleton that her flesh looked as though it might rip. I couldn't understand how her lengthy braid of wild gray hair didn't tip her over and snap her in half.

Melba spun around and flashed a big grin when she saw Tommy. "If it isn't the local delinquent!" she laughed. Several of her teeth were missing, which I suspected could be a result of her condition. "It's good to see you, Tommy. You show up every year just like my hay fever."

"Yep, that's me," he laughed. "I'm everybody's favorite allergy. Melba, meet my friend, Rainy."

"Hello there, Rainy. Didn't I see you here with an elderly man last night?"

"Yes, ma'am, we were here."

"Just as I thought! You passed me by over near the big wheel. I remember how his silver hair and your long blond hair caught the light. I'm pleased to meet you, dear."

"Thank you. So you run this ride?"

"Melba is also a performer," Tommy announced. "She can pass her body through a tennis racket."

"Childhood worms," she nodded. "I'm one of the Anatomical Wonders, but I run rides because we're shorthanded," she explained while offering a slender hand. When we shook, I was careful not to press too hard for fear of breaking her bones.

"There are still a few empty cars on the ride, so how about if you two take a spin? My treat. Just pretend you're pressing a ticket in my hand and then go grab a swing."

With great drama, we feigned an exchange of tickets before running to our separate cars. I had never ridden the Tilt-A-Whirl before, so I was full of anticipation. Once we started spinning, I experienced a lightness I hadn't felt since everything went topsy-turvy with my parents. As the cars spun around and the platform rose and fell, the breeze swept my ponytail off my neck, and I felt as though I were flying. With each spin of the car, I slid back and forth across my seat like a bead on an abacus wire.

Tommy and I called out to each other every time his car twirled past mine, and I laughed until I was hoarse. We rode four times before the ride began to fill up with paying customers, so we thanked Melba and bid her goodbye before heading down the midway, pushing and shoving each other, as giddy as two kookaburras.

We stopped at booths along the way to watch the action, cheering on the players who were determined to win a prize. Tommy, who was a frequent carnival interloper, knew the names of many of the workers who ran the games. Several carnies let us compete just for fun and to help draw a crowd. Because we were playing for free, we didn't get a prize if we won a game, but we still had a great time.

One huge and strange-looking man who was repairing the Bumper Cars nodded to Tommy and grunted. His face was badly scarred, so when he smiled, his jaw contorted, and the damaged tissue puckered around his misshapen cheekbones in irregular pockets of shiny shin. What was even more unsettling was that he was staring at me, as though *I* were the odd one.

"Let's move on," I whispered to Tommy. "That guy is giving me the willies."

"Oh, that's just how Bugg looks," Tommy assured me. "Melba told me that the poor guy was in a bad construction accident, and he broke a lot of the bones in his face and skull. His eyes look like they're staring at you, but he can't even see out of one of them, hence the name Bugg. He's harmless though."

"Why does he grunt?"

"He can't communicate much because the accident supposedly damaged the speech center of his brain. Even though he's good at fixing things, he can't get outside work now. Everyone assumes he's mentally deficient, although he isn't. But some parts of his brain never healed, so the carnies took him in. He's hard to look at and understand, but he's strong as an ox. Melba says he's harmless."

Harmless or not, I was relieved when Tommy agreed to

move on. After we left Bugg, we strolled to the burlesque show because Tommy wanted to watch the women dance. It was much later at night than when my grandpa and I had attended, so the crowd around the burlesque tent was even bigger than it had been the preceding night.

I noticed how bright Tommy's eyes became as he watched what he referred to as the "hoochie-coochie girls" parading across the stage. Even though I was fairly inexperienced with boys, Tommy's reactions fascinated me. I liked how he looked at the women, and I sensed we both were moving closer to a time when we both would leave our innocence behind.

After we stood there for a few minutes, Tommy noticed an older man staring at me. "I don't like the way that guy keeps looking our way," he whispered. "It ain't polite."

"Is he one of our neighbors?" I questioned nervously. "If he is, and if he tells anyone he saw me here with you, I'll be deader than a smoked turkey."

Tommy suddenly grabbed me by the arm and dragged me in the opposite direction of the burlesque show. "I don't recognize him, but there are some dodgy people here late at night, so let's get you home," he said.

"Tommy, you and I are the same age. Stop treating me like a child."

"I'm treating you like someone whose grandpa will kill me if anything happens to you. Com'on, Rainy, we've had a good time. We can come back again tomorrow night."

"Do you mean that? This is one of the best nights of my life, and I'll only leave if you promise we'll come again," I demanded.

"I promise. But please, let's go before someone notices we're missing."

As we crawled back under the fence, I felt a firm grasp on

my shoulder. "I'm moving as fast as I can, Tommy," I grumbled as I proceeded with my belly crawl.

When I got halfway under the wire, I lifted my head. I was surprised and confused to see that Tommy was much further ahead of me than I realized. The moonlight illuminated him as he turned back to see where I was. He stopped moving, and then suddenly a look of terror darkened his face, causing me to freeze in place. Still on the ground, I glanced to my right and spotted a pair of dark work boots. Someone was standing next to me.

6

NIAGARA

In a panic, I tried to crawl clear of the fence to make my escape, but the wire pressed down on my back, holding me in place. I dug my fingers into the soft earth and attempted to thrust myself forward, but the grip on my shoulder prevented me from moving.

"Run, Rainy!" Tommy yelled. "Get up and run!" As I lay on the ground, I felt the hand grasp my shoulder tighter. "Please don't hurt me," I whimpered.

"Up," the voice commanded.

When I lifted my head, I was terrified to see a large man hovering over me. I couldn't see his face in the dark, but by his height and size, I knew I was trapped. As my eyes finally adjusted, I realized I was being held captive by Bugg, the menacing carny from the Bumper Car area. He was breathing heavily, and he had a crowbar in his hand.

Before I could plead for mercy, Bugg suddenly pulled me backward by my feet to the carnival side of the fence. "Go for help, Tommy!" I screamed as the hulking man dragged me back toward the midway.

———

Bugg kept a firm grasp on my arm as he dragged me along the fence in the darkness, far from the midway lights so we would not be seen. I struggled to scream again, but only a choking sound crawled out of my throat. It was like screaming in a nightmare. I could hear the screams in my head, but no one else could hear me. I had never experienced such terror. "Please," I whispered, "please."

"No scream," Bugg grunted as he dragged me closer and closer to the front exit of the carnival, all the while staying along the edge of the fence in the dark. By then, my face was streaming with tears, and I was choking back vomit. I was sure he was going to kill me.

Suddenly, as we got closer to the front entrance, I spotted Officer Montelongo from our neighborhood. I recognized him from the dance hall, where I had seen him once with his wife. Montelongo was pacing back and forth while checking his watch.

When Bugg saw him, he paused, loosening his grip on me. In that instant, I seized my chance to escape. I elbowed Bugg sharply in the stomach, and then I ran to Officer Montelongo and threw myself at him.

"That man is trying to kidnap me!" I screamed. I was shaking and sobbing as I clutched Montelongo tightly and buried my face in his chest. When I turned to point at Bugg, I was astounded to see that he didn't even attempt to run.

"Settle down, now. Everything is okay," the officer said as he tried to calm me.

"He was taking me with him!"

"The carnival is small, so he'd have a hard time hiding you," he smiled.

"Why aren't you taking this seriously? He could dye my

skin brown with walnut stain and no one would be able to identify me!"

"You have quite the imagination. I'm the one who sent Bugg for you. When I showed him your photo, he indicated that he recognized you."

"You sent him to kidnap me?"

"Rainy, slow down. Take a few breaths and just listen. No one is kidnapping you. I'm here on police business."

"Police business? Are you arresting me just because I snuck into the carnival without paying? Are you booking me?"

"Booking you? Rainy, I'm sorry to laugh, but you read too many books. I'm not arresting you."

"Isn't it fraud to enter without a ticket?"

"Yes, but I doubt you will end up on a chain gang if that's another thought that's rumbling around in that head of yours, although a chain gang might do your friend Tommy some good."

"Is Tommy in trouble too?"

"Not with us, but maybe with his dad. My partner drove around to pick him up on the other side of the woods, so he'll make sure Tommy gets home safely. But I suspected you might be here ... along with other delinquents from the neighborhood who sneak in here every night."

"You know about that?"

"Of course. It's a summer ritual. I figured Bugg knew where you kids slip in and out. That's dishonest, you know, but I don't plan to 'book you' this time."

"So I'm not going to juvenile detention?"

"Not unless you continue to hang out with Tommy. I'm here because your grandfather called us. He's looking for you, and he suspected you might be here."

"Why is Grandpa looking for me? He's supposed to be in bed."

"So are you, young lady. And it's way past curfew for kids your age. I see my partner is back with the squad car, so please thank Bugg, and let's get you home. Oh, and you should probably apologize to him for clobbering him."

"Thank you, Bugg. I'm sorry I was so afraid of you," I said, contritely, "and I'm sorry I punched you in the gut."

As Bugg nodded, he held out his hand to me. I was still afraid of him, and I couldn't stop trembling, but when I felt his huge hand in mine, I was surprised at how warm and comforting it was. Suddenly, he seemed more human and less like a masked monster.

"I truly am sorry," I said shamefully.

After I turned to follow Officer Montelongo, a new dread set in. I knew I was about to face a heap of trouble at home. Although Grandpa seldom got angry, there was no way for me to escape a serious grounding.

"Maybe I should have taken my chances on a chain gang," I mumbled to Officer Montelongo as we drove the short distance to my house. But when the police car turned onto my street, I realized that what I had once thought would be a harmless escapade had turned out to be far more consequential than I ever could have imagined.

———

There was a cluster of glaring lights in front of our garage apartment that were as bright as those of the carnival. The lights slashed the darkness, creating a macabre backdrop to the action in the driveway. An ambulance lurked, its back doors open like the mouth of a predator about to swallow the body that was being fed to it on a stainless steel gurney.

As soon as I jumped out of the car, Grandpa came running

down the driveway. "Gramps I'm so sorry!" I sobbed. "What's happening? What's happening?"

"Rainy, I need you to be brave. Go to your father before they take him away. His time has come."

Grandpa pounded on the side of the ambulance just as the attendant was closing the doors. "That's my son in there," he yelled. "Open the damn door!"

As soon as the attendant opened the door again, Grandpa grabbed me by the arm and pulled me up into the ambulance with him. I stared at my father, who looked like an apparition in the harsh white light. "Daddy, don't go!" I screamed.

Grandpa moved in closer to my dad. "Hold on, son," Grandpa pleaded.

"I can't, Pops. I'm sorry," my father whispered.

"Dammit, do something to help him!" Grandpa yelled at the medic.

My father reached up to pull Grandpa closer to him. "No more," Dad whispered. "I love you and Rainy Marie to the ends of the earth," he smiled sadly. His eyes went blank, like the last frame on a roll of film, and then his eyelids closed, shutting out Grandpa and me forever.

Just then, the siren blared as the ambulance backed out of the driveway. Grandpa and I draped our bodies across my father in our hopeless attempt to keep him warm. But it didn't matter anymore. My dad had gone to Niagara.

7

THE TURNING POINT

Somehow, Grandpa and I managed to get each other through the days that followed my Dad's death. Primrose was the first to show up, and her loving embrace was the only thing that convinced me that I would survive the entire event. John Joe and Grandpa's other friends from Jukie's came around often. Most of the visitors from Jukie's had never met my dad, although a few of them remembered him from his days at Eatwell Bakery.

Our house was teeming with neighbors bearing casseroles and Bundt cakes. Charles, my dad's former boss from Eatwell, dropped by with a box of cupcakes. When Charles apologized to Grandpa about their altercation at the bakery, my grandfather said he was sorry too, and told him to just forget the whole incident because he had finally realized that my dad was not in any shape to be holding down a job. Gramps also apologized for taking out his anger on a defenseless blueberry pie, which gave them both a chuckle.

One of our visitors was Officer Montelongo, who, like me,

had not expected to find an ambulance in the driveway when he brought me home from the carnival the night my father died. I remembered how helpful he had been in keeping things under control as neighbors rushed over to see what was going on.

When Officer Montelongo arrived to pay his respects, he made me giggle by asking how my life on a chain gang was going. I didn't know if it was appropriate to laugh, but Gramps assured me that any form of merriment would make my father happy. He explained that something had gone wrong inside my dad's brain that had slowly extinguished his ability to feel happiness, so laughter would help fill the emptiness that a chemical imbalance and life itself had left in place of my dad.

Tommy also stopped by one afternoon with his parents. "I'm so sorry, Rainy," he whispered to me. "I should never have taken you to the carnival that night. My dad said I'm grounded until I'm twenty-five or maybe even fifty because you should have been home when everything happened."

Of course, I immediately started crying. That's when Tommy's father, who I can only assume was trying to help, kept saying to me, "Shh, Rainy, shush now. Don't cry, honey."

"Please don't shush her," Grandpa said. "Rainy, you cry as much as you need to. Sorrow is an expression of love, and love has no bounds, so neither should your tears. Let the teardrops help wash away your pain."

I didn't believe the pain would ever go away.

———

Those days of adjusting to my father's absence were hard, so after three weeks, Grandpa suggested that we go to the dance hall for an hour or two. "Rainy, music is like water because it sustains life. You and I need to hear some music again, don't you think?"

I knew he was right, and I wanted to see Primrose because she was the only person who could make both of us feel like life would one day be normal again. We were preparing to leave when heard a knock. If we had known what was about to happen, we would never have answered the door.

Standing on our front porch was an officious-looking woman in a brown suit. At first, we thought she was there to pay her respects, but everything changed when she presented a paper and her business card to Grandpa. "I'm sorry to disturb you, but I am afraid I'm here on official business, Mr. Merrill," she said somewhat tentatively. She glanced at me as I moved next to my grandfather.

"What kind of business?"

"Respectfully, sir, I must inform you that your son's death certificate has been filed by the coroner, and because he was the only person on the lease for this apartment, you will need to abandon the premises as soon as possible."

"That won't be necessary," Grandpa informed her. "We can switch the lease over to my name. I know we are losing my son's disability insurance, but with my Social Security and the money I make from landscaping, we can make ends meet without it."

"According to this affidavit, you have fallen three months behind in your rent payments."

"I believe that's correct, ma'am, but we've had a lot of medical bills, and most recently, we've had to pay funeral bills. We can catch up."

"My sincere condolences. Unfortunately, sir, I do not make the decisions on these matters. And the situation is a bit more complicated than the question of rent. I don't think you read my card, but I'm from the state Children's Aid Society, and the document I gave you is a temporary court order."

Gramps looked stunned as he examined the document. "This can't possibly be accurate," he mumbled.

"Because you are elderly, the State received notification of your court-ruled eviction. For your protection, they reviewed the case to verify that the eviction is lawful, and based on the delinquent payments, they concluded that it is.

"However, while evaluating the case, they also discovered that you are not a legal relative of the underage girl who lives here with you, so they turned the matter over to the New York Society for the Prevention of Cruelty to Children. I'm sorry to say, but it has been determined that the girl can no longer remain in your home without a legal guardian."

"Ma'am, you are gravely mistaken. This is my granddaughter." Gramps yanked me to his side and wrapped a protective arm around my shoulders.

"Sir, we know your recently deceased son was not your legal child, and therefore, this young lady is not your legal granddaughter. We cannot allow someone who is not related to a minor child to house them unless it's a proper foster placement."

"Then I will foster her."

"That is a long process, and you will have no chance of being approved, not only because there is no female adult in the household but also because within three days, you will no longer have a home. I am very sorry. Although I do not make these decisions, I am assigned with the unhappy task of carrying them out."

"What is she saying, Gramps?" I interrupted. "Tell her you are my grandfather—that my dad was your son." When I looked at the woman, I felt a dark curtain falling around us. "I think you should leave!" I yelled.

Grandpa placed his hand on my shoulder in an attempt to keep me calm. "My son was the only child I ever had," Grandpa said quietly. He looked down at his feet, and his shoulders slumped as though weighted with defeat.

As I sensed something was truly amiss, panic set in. "Tell her, Gramps," I demanded. "Make her go away."

I had never seen my grandfather look so crestfallen. He shook his head from side to side before gazing back up at her. "I took my son in when he was seven years old. He was a street urchin. He came around, begging for work and something to eat. My wife Evie and I learned to love him, and we gave him a home. He has never been anything to me but my one and only child--my son."

"But you never legally adopted him, Mr. Merrill. And he did have one living relative. His uncle was looking for him for years."

"His uncle was the drunk who beat him unmercifully and threw him out to live on the streets when he was only seven years old! Seven! If that depraved reprobate was looking for him, the only reason would be to use my son to steal liquor. He didn't even give the boy food!"

"I agree that is tragic. Fortunately, the uncle has passed on. But you never adopted him legally, Mr. Merrill, and as I mentioned, there is a correct process."

"There is also right versus wrong."

"Well, sir, then you should have done it the right way."

"Ma'am, you don't understand because you're too young. Times were much more challenging back then. It was just after WWI, and there were a lot of children living on the streets who had no families and no means of survival. During the war, we barely had money to eat, so there was no possible way we could afford lawyers to go through a legal process. Our only 'process' was to help a child survive and endure. We had very little ourselves, but those of us who provided homes saved lives."

"But Mr. Merrill, he wasn't a dog you could just take in."

"Would you treat a dog better? Would you leave a parent-less child who was starving out on the street? Evie and I loved him. He was our son. He was our life, and no paperwork can ever change that!"

"Unfortunately, the State of New York does not see things that way. Although I agree with you, I also have to do my job. Per my instructions, I will return in twenty-four hours to take the girl with me."

"Take me where?" I demanded. "You're crazy if you believe I'm going anywhere with you. I'm staying right here with my grandfather."

"There are nice people who will give you a home, Miss Bryant," she answered.

"'Bryant'? What kind of a place do you work for?" I snapped. "You don't even have the right person. My name is Lorraine Merrill!"

"Your father's legal surname was Bryant, not Merrill. Your name is Lorraine Bryant."

I was stunned. She was talking about someone I had never even met. As I searched for the words to respond, she turned her focus back to Grandpa.

"The girl doesn't even know who she is. Do you understand the damage that has been done, Mr. Merrill?"

Gramps set his jaw and spoke through clenched teeth. His gaze was steely and his shoulders had grown rigid. "She knows who she is. She is a Merrill, just as her father—my son—was a Merrill. Do you understand the damage that *you* are doing? Rainy is my granddaughter, and her home is with me. And you are not taking her anywhere."

"Mr. Merrill, you can't fight this. I will be back tomorrow

with some officers from the State. Please have her possessions packed to avoid any sort of altercation. We will also send a police car around tonight to check up on her. Please allow them entry. Again, I truly apologize. I will take my leave now."

After we slammed the door behind her, we stood silently, staring at each other in shock. Then Grandpa started to cry, which was almost as devastating as losing my dad.

8

CIVIL DISOBEDIENCE

"Gramps, I don't care about a piece of paper. You are my one and only grandfather, and you always will be. I'm never going to live with anyone but you."

"But sweetheart, they're going to return for you."

"I am not going with them! Aren't we a team? And didn't you teach me to fight for what is right and just? You know this isn't right! Let's just leave here. When they show up, we'll be gone."

"We could get arrested if we flee? I'm the one whom they would take into custody, but then you would end up in foster care, anyway. It's too risky, Rainy."

"I'm not afraid to take our chances if you're not afraid."

Grandpa closed his eyes and ran his hand through his hair. "I don't understand how they think that breaking up a family is a means of doing good."

"You have always said that some people value rules over justice and common sense. Do you think Primrose would let us live with her?"

"I'm sure she would, but there is no way we can get

anybody else involved. Technically I broke the law, so Prim could get in trouble for taking me in."

"Broke the law by saving my father? But you said that some things deemed legal are not always right ... like how Prim can be refused service in the same restaurants where we can eat. You also told me sometimes we must stand up to authority with peaceful resistance."

"Yes, yes I did say that."

"Then let's resist, Gramps. Please don't let them make me live with strangers. I'm begging you."

"I will never let that happen, Rainy."

I watched as Gramps paced back and forth, trying to determine our next move. He constantly rubbed his forehead as if his head was throbbing.

"Gramps, please," I whispered. "Let's go somewhere far away. There's nothing left to keep us here."

I thought he would never answer. Finally, he looked at me the way he always did when there was no more room for discussion. "Rainy, grab your things."

"Are you going with me?"

"Yes. You are my grandchild, and you're not going anywhere alone. But we have to hurry. Put your most important possessions into a pillowcase that you can throw over your shoulder. Take only what you need. We must leave tonight before they come back."

———

Within one hour, we were ready to go. I grabbed the framed photo of my mom and dad off the mantle, and then Grandpa turned off the lights and locked the doors. When we got to the bottom of the steps of our garage apartment, he whispered,

"It's dark, and there's not much moonlight tonight, Rainy, but we have to move quickly."

"Which way are we heading?"

"Down Jennings and then down Elm Street to the woods to the shallow part of the creek you showed me. We can wade across. No one will see us in the woods, so that way we'll get a head start."

It was so dark that night that it was very difficult to see, but I felt safer in the shadows. I instinctively knew where the shallow places in the creek were, so once we got down the embankment to the creek, we took off our shoes and I led Grandpa across.

When we reached the other side, I was startled to see a man hunkered down in the grass, drying off his feet. Grandpa reached for me just as I covered my mouth to keep from screaming. Although there was very little moonlight, when he looked up, I realized by his misshapen head and face that it was Bugg. He seemed just as startled as we were, so I held one finger over my lips to signal for him to stay silent.

"Rainy, watch out!" Grandpa yanked me away from Bugg and shoved me behind him to protect me.

"He's okay, Gramps," I whispered in the dark. "He's Officer Montelongo's friend."

"Howdy do, sir," Grandpa whispered politely. "We don't mean to disturb. We're just passing through."

Just as we were putting our shoes back on, we saw the lights of a police car at the top of the embankment, and within seconds, another vehicle pulled up next to the first squad car. "Don't be afraid," Grandpa whispered, "just hurry." I was already in such a state of panic that I dropped my shoe in the tall grass.

"Gramps, I lost my shoe," I whispered. "And I don't have

another pair with me!" Although we pawed through the grass for several minutes, our search was fruitless.

"We can't use the flashlight," Gramps said into my ear. With one arm, he flailed around inside his pillowcase until he retracted another pair of socks. "Put these over your socks for extra padding. We've got to keep moving. We'll find extra shoes for you as soon as we can."

As we were heading up the hillside, a spotlight suddenly lit up the woods. I didn't know if the police were looking for us, or for Bugg and any other carny workers who might be bathing in the creek.

Bugg was making his way through the woods ahead of us, so we followed his lead up the embankment, staying where the grass was tall and darting behind trees whenever the light swept the hill in our direction. I could hear Gramps by my side, panting rapidly. My heart was pounding so hard that my chest hurt, but I kept going.

When we got to the top of the hill, Bugg ran toward the fence that surrounded the carnival. Gramps and I went in the opposite direction along the edge of the grounds toward Main Street, but the searchlight grew closer just as Gramps stopped to place his hand on his chest.

"Keep going, Gramps. Please!"

"I can't go on, honey," Gramps was panting so hard he scared me. "You keep running. Go to John Joe's. He'll take you to Primrose."

"No! You have to--"

"Psst!"

The sound startled us. We both stood still and listened. Then, just as the spotlight swept the area, we heard the sound again.

"Psst!"

Gramps and I turned in the direction of the voice. Bugg had

chased after Gramps and me and was calling to us from inside the carnival grounds. He was holding up a piece of the wire fence, signaling to us to crawl under. "Come," he whispered as he struggled to enunciate his words. "Now!"

Gramps held back, but I knew Bugg was trying to save us. I nudged Gramps forward.

We crawled under the fencing until we safely reached the other side within the confines of the carnival. The warm lights that greeted us were friendlier than the cold and harsh spotlight that continued to search the hillside for fugitives, which is what we now were.

After we got to our feet, we didn't know where to go until Bugg made a sweeping gesture of welcome. Gramps and I stood for a moment in silence as Bugg offered us refuge within the mysterious world of traveling carnies.

9

GREENIES

As Grandpa and I followed Bugg through the carnival, our eyes darted about, constantly wary of any new threats. Bugg led us to a group of wagons behind the brightly lit amusement area. As we got closer, I realized that the wagons were converted railroad cars mounted on heavy trailer bases with wheels. The cars had rows of windows along the sides, and each was decorated with wood panels painted in kaleidoscope colors.

When we arrived at a red and yellow car, Bugg held up one hand as a gesture for us to wait. We watched as he climbed up the three steps and opened the door, exposing a studio that reminded me of a storybook chalet. There was a neatly made bed built into an alcove at the back, with a floral patchwork quilt that looked like a garden. Next to the bed was an inviting stuffed chair, its rolled arms covered with white crocheted doilies. Someone had strung colored twinkle lights throughout the interior and draped the rows of windows with fringed scarves in vivid patterns.

Off to one side was a tiny kitchen area with a small refrigerator, a sink, and a cooktop. On the counter, a large bowl and an oversized pottery water pitcher were placed next to a neat stack of dishes.

I was most interested in the shelves above the kitchen counter. Instead of being stacked with kitchen paraphernalia, the shelves were covered with volumes of books and an old kewpie doll.

Bugg looked massive in proportion to the small space. After he opened an old trunk that served as a coffee table, he shuffled through its contents. He searched for several minutes before withdrawing a pair of sneakers. Bugg glanced at my feet and then back at the sneakers before he shyly offered them to me.

Touched by his thoughtfulness, I nodded in thanks and slipped them on while Grandpa shook his hand in gratitude. The shoes were only slightly too big for me, so I bunched up the toes of my socks to fill the excess space. Bugg then gestured for us to continue to follow him.

"Backyard," he said, pointing to a row of trucks and vans in the back that were illuminated by strings of overhead lights.

We hadn't yet reached the vans when an unusual-looking gentleman came up alongside us. He was only about as tall as I, with a protuberant belly, very short arms, and almost no neck. He wasn't quite small enough to be considered a dwarf or a midget, but he was strangely misshapen, with a large forehead and one gold tooth that flashed in the light. He nodded to us and then turned to Bugg. "You brought me gazoonies, big man? I'm afraid the kid is too young."

Bugg shook his head and struggled to communicate. "H-h-hey Rube."

"Ah, I see." The odd man looked us over carefully. "'Hey, Rube' is how we call for help. The big guy is trying to say you've got trouble."

Bugg nodded. "Good folk," he uttered.

The guy shoved his tweed newsboy hat back farther on his head to get a better look at us. I wasn't sure whether to take him seriously until Bugg said, "Boss Jones."

Grandpa held out his hand to introduce us. "Mr. Jones, we're not here to cause trouble, although we've had a little of our own. I am Reese Merrill, and this is my granddaughter, Rainy. If we can stay till morning, we'd be very grateful."

Jones eyed Grandpa up and down before shaking his hand. "You wanted by the cops?"

"I believe we may be. We will leave now if you like."

"Hold on now." He then looked directly at me. "Young lady, are you with this man by choice?"

"Yes, sir. He's my Gramps. He is the only family I have, and a child services group is trying to take him away from me because of a paperwork error. But he has always been my grandfather."

"Yeah? How do we know he doesn't make you say that?"

"Wait, look here!" I said, as I reached into my pillowcase duffel bag and pulled out my library card. "See! We have the same last name—Merrill."

As Jones examined the card, he took off his hat and scratched his bald pate. "It seems Bugg trusts you. And if the big man vouches for you, then you're with us now. And providing we don't get no trouble here, you can stay for as long as you need to until we jump to our new location in two weeks."

"We'll figure out something by then, sir," Gramps assured him, although his voice didn't sound too convincing.

"We could use some help. I lost two people this week who got copped for stealing, even though they were just shopping in the wrong place. So they won't be coming back this season, and old Marny had to leave after she lost her hand while setting up the Caterpillar ride. You can stay in one of their rail cars. We call 'em wagons because of the wheels. Bugg can show you around while you lie low."

"Thank you, Jones," Gramps said. We just need a bed for Rainy."

"We got plenty of beds. Bugg, please have Melba give Rainy a hand settling in."

"We can pay for our keep," Gramps offered.

"To us, trust is more important than money. We don't take to cowboys, but you look like honest people. I have a nose for it. You can stay the night for free. If you want to stay longer, are you willing to work to earn your keep?"

"Oh, yes," I spoke up. "Grandpa is super fast and accurate with numbers, and I'm a fast learner too. I already met Melba, and I'd be happy to help her run the rides."

"Hmm ... let me think about this. In the meantime, you get settled in and then go on back and see Reno in the cookhouse so he can get you some grub. Don't mind his missing fingers. He always leaves something floating in the chili. 'Gives new meaning to finger food, right?"

Grandpa and I weren't sure how to react until Jones started chuckling. Bugg did too, but his laugh was more like a heaving cough. "You'd be surprised at how good our fare is."

"That's kind of you," Grandpa said.

"By the way, Reese, considering your circumstances, you should never mention your surname to anyone, understand? Your new last name is Ford, like the car. That should be easy to remember. Can you also remember that, Rainy?"

"Yes, Mr. Jones."

"Good. And it's just Jones. Be forewarned that cops often hang out at the entrance, so stay away from the arch. That way, if anyone comes asking, we ain't never seen you two."

The peculiar boss man then spun on his heel and headed toward the lights.

———

Bugg took us back to the caravan area to the mysterious but magical wagon that was like a giant dollhouse on wheels where we had stopped for shoes. "Miss," Bugg pointed, indicating that the wagon would be my quarters.

Our soft-spoken guide towered over Gramps as he led him to the wagon directly across from mine. When he opened the door, I could see that it was very similar to mine. The interior of his wagon was decorated with a lot of khaki and white, so it was subtle but very tranquil.

"This will do just fine," Gramps nodded. "Thank you, Bugg."

Bugg pulled back the bedspread to show Gramps the bedding. "Squeaks clean. Eat now."

We left our few possessions in the wagons and then traipsed after him, avoiding the amusement area. The carnival was packed with visitors who seemed as carefree as I had once been. From afar, I spotted Mr. DiGiovanni near the shooting gallery, but then he disappeared into the crowd along with everything else that was familiar to me.

I hadn't had time to give it much thought, but my heart was slowly acknowledging many painful endings. I would never see my dad again. And it was likely I would never see my friends again or all the places that were part of the person who used to be Rainy--my brick school that smelled like finger paint, Tommy and his old golden retriever, Jukie's with the root beer-colored floors, Primrose, who was like a fairy godmother, the musty public library, the winding creek, and the rows of maples and elms that hung in a green arch over my street. Even my name was gone.

The tears burned at the corners of my eyes again, but I brushed them away. As I walked next to Gramps, I wondered if he was feeling the same thing. He once told me it was sometimes hard for old people to start over, and yet he had to say his goodbyes too, and he was willing to do it all for me. I reached out and took his hand as we walked into our new life.

10

FREAKS

We stayed in the shadows until we arrived at the cook wagon, which was a food concession wagon surrounded by a temporary outdoor kitchen under a light-strung tent. Long picnic tables dotted the area where a group of carnies were just sitting down to dinner.

When Bugg introduced us to Reno the cook, the leathery-faced carny just grunted and passed three metal bowls through the service window. We then helped ourselves to chili and cornbread at the service table before sitting down with a few workers, who eyed us curiously.

"Good evening, everyone," Grandpa said properly. "We're just passing through, but we thank you for sharing your supper with us."

"Well, ain't you polite, you silver fox! I'm Viv, known as Vivian the Voluptuous Vixen, and I don't share my supper with nobody," she laughed.

Viv was the largest human being I had ever seen in my life. When she laughed, the entire table moved. I had to clutch my bowl of stew to keep from wearing it. Her features seemed to have receded into her face, which reminded me of an inner tube, but her eyes lit up when she smiled. I liked her immediately.

Next to her was a Negro man who I was afraid to look at. He didn't have a discernable face. Unlike Bugg, where it was apparent that he had suffered some sort of accident or war injury, the Negro man had huge, fleshy growths all over him.

His face was a cluster of scaly mushroom-like mounds so enormous that his head was almost twice as large as a normal human head. Distorted beyond anything recognizable, his face had no definable nose, and the openings that served as his eyes were askew. The outcropping of skin growth on his neck was so large there was no separation between his head and neck. It was apparent by the fit of his clothes that the warty protrusions covered much of his body as well.

He said a word to Bugg, but I couldn't make out what he was saying. The two men seemed to have a private language of grunts and gestures. I noticed how the gentleman with the growths covered his mouth when he ate. As he chewed, his mouth turned like a washing machine, and he had difficulty keeping his food from spilling out. Each bite seemed to be an arduous task.

"What's your name, girly girl?" The question came from a young man who was sitting at the end of the table. He didn't look to be much older than I was.

"I'm Rainy," I answered. "And this is Gramps."

"Pleased to meet ya.' People call me Sim, which is short for Simian 'cause I can swing like a monkey. I call it flying. And that there fellow sitting next to you is Easy Earl. We call him that because he's such a gentle fella. Earl is part of the Freak Show like Viv. In our world, freaks are special."

"I'm extra special because there is a lot more of me, and I'm gorgeous," Viv guffawed. "We have a saying around here, 'True

BEYOND THE HOLE IN THE FENCE

beauty is in the unique,' and we're all unique. Earl, don't be shy. Say hello to our guests."

When I lifted my eyes to look at Earl, he nodded politely. He then noticed my grandfather's outstretched hand. Earl hesitated before lifting his hand, which looked like a baseball mitt. Grandpa didn't flinch. I knew Earl's deformed limb must have felt strange and off-putting to touch, but Gramps never let on.

Sim wiped his mouth on his hand and continued talking. "Viv is right. Earl is one of the most attractive people here, in a Salvador Dali-like way. And I am the most mobile. Because of my talent at flying, I scale the big rides when they need fixin'. Come to think about it, I need help with Big Eli if you two are looking for work."

"Who is Big Eli?"

"Y'all must be greenies. Big Eli is what townies call a Ferris wheel. He got his name because they're constructed by the Eli Bridge Company in Jacksonville, Illinois, my hometown. We are all mighty proud of that. The wheel we've got here is old, so it has been breaking down a lot recently. Gramps, are you any good with mechanics?"

"Not so much, Sim. We don't know how long we'll be staying, but as long as I'm here, I'm happy to help you out in any way I can."

"That'll be mighty fine. Folks say I'm chatty, but I'm easy to work with. I'm happy-go-lucky because we all have so much to be thankful for."

"I'm thankful for this delicious stew," Viv agreed, nodding enthusiastically. "Reno, can you bring me another bowl?" she yelled over her shoulder to the cook. Reno let out a loud grunt as he began spooning more stew into a bowl.

Sim laughed. "Reno is a darn good cook. He pretends to be grouchy, but that's just all for show. He wants us to think twice before sneaking into his supplies. I hope you're around long enough to join us for our Sunday gathering. We have some folks who sing gospel music that will send chills up and down your spine, and Viv sometimes joins in."

"That sounds enticing," Gramps said.

"Maybe I'll catch you there. Welcome to you both. Catch y'all later."

With that, Sim pressed his hands on the table and used the strength of his arms to elevate himself until he was standing on his hands on the tabletop. I was shocked and unsettled to see that he was missing his body from the bottom of his torso down. As he walked on his hands along the table, no one bothered to look or even move their dishes out of the way.

Sim deftly avoided bumping into anything, even as he stopped to snatch a piece of cornbread off Viv's plate. When he got to the end of the table, he then reached out to a pole that held the tent canvas. I stared in awe as he swung from pole to pole before disappearing into the night.

As I watched in wonder, I sensed that my world was about to explode with events that, until that night, had been beyond my imagination.

11

WANTED

I slept fitfully on our first evening there. Despite not knowing for sure what my grandfather's plans were, I assumed we would head for another safe place at daybreak.

Even though everyone was very kind and welcoming, Grandpa slept on the floor of my wagon to make sure I was safe. His concern was unnecessary, because Bugg sat outside in a chair most of the night, sometimes even marching back and forth as if he were guarding the Tomb of the Unknown Soldier.

As soon as the sun rose and I exited my wagon, I saw Grandpa carrying two cups of coffee on his way back from the cook wagon. He offered one to Bugg, who was just stirring after a quick nap in the chair.

"Good morning, Miss Ford," Gramps greeted me as he threw me an orange.

"Are we still safe?" I whispered.

Before he could answer, Melba, the skinny woman whom I met with Tommy, walked up to greet us. She was accompanied by a dwarf-size woman who had a very tiny head with a dramatically sloped forehead. Atop her head was a knot of hair that seemed to have been squeezed out like toothpaste from a tube. The topknot emphasized her undersized skull. I knew from carnival flyers I had seen that she was considered a "pinhead."

"Good morning," Melba said as she got closer. "Do you remember me?"

"Yes, you're Melba. I'm Rainy Mer-"

"Rainy Ford," she said, cutting me off before I could say my name. "Jones told me you were here. This is Dotty. Say hello, Dotty." Dotty flashed an impish grin and then did a dramatic curtsy. Although she looked older than me, she seemed very childlike. "Stay right next to me, Dotty," Melba ordered. "Don't you go running off, missy. Bugg and I don't feel like chasing you today. We are going to show these kind people around the show."

Grandpa immediately introduced himself. "Thank you, Melba, but I think we'll be moving on sometime today. We sure appreciate your hospitality."

"Gramps, you and your granddaughter shouldn't leave just yet. It's too dangerous."

Grandpa seemed caught off-guard. Although he was unaware of how much she knew, I sensed he was unsure of our surroundings.

"Melba, I don't think this is the best environment for a young girl. We're strangers to you and to your way of life. I worry about her safety."

"It's safer in here than out there."

"Then why did Bugg sit up most of the night just to protect us?"

Melba looked at Bugg and then back at us. "Jones is kinda psychic. Last night, after you fell asleep, the boss had a bad feeling, so he told Bugg to watch over you. Bugg wasn't protecting you from us carnies. He was protecting you from outsiders."

Melba reached into her pocket and pulled out a flyer to show Gramps. "These are being distributed throughout the area."

Gramps and I were both stunned to see a notice with our photos on it announcing that Grandpa was wanted for abduction, and anyone who had any information should call the police immediately. The flyer screamed the words so loudly that Grandpa dropped the paper and reeled back as though he had been shot.

"I found the flyer this morning posted at the entry arch. Actually, there were several. I recognized the photo of Rainy because I saw her here with you one evening, and again the following night with Tommy. It was clear there was some sort of mistake, so I immediately showed the notice to Jones who said you had taken refuge here on the lot. After he caught me up to speed, he told me to find you and warn you."

"Is Gramps going to be arrested?" I asked.

"Not if we can prevent it. But as long as the police are looking for you, I would advise you to stay out of sight with us until the carnival moves out of Endicott. Early this morning, we got the word out to the others that for the time being, you're one of us."

Gramps stared at the Wanted Notice for a long time before he finally looked at me and said, "I cannot believe I'm a wanted man. I should turn myself in so this horrible situation doesn't get worse."

"No, Gramps, you can't. Please don't do that. They'll take me away from you and place me in a home. Can we just stay here a while longer while we figure things out?"

"The girl makes sense," Melba said. As she spoke, she struggled to keep hold of Dotty's hand to prevent her from breaking free. "Get some breakfast, and then Bugg will bring you over to my wagon so we can change how you look while he catches up on his sleep."

"Guard outside." Bugg painstakingly pronounced the word.

"Okay, Bugg. You can stand watch while I do my magic. Rainy, we need to cut your hair, and maybe pluck your brows and add some lipstick to make you look older. Hats will help too. Gramps, we're going to shave off your mustache and darken your hair quite a bit. The silver color is beautiful, but it catches the light, and we don't want anything to draw more attention to you. Orders from Jones."

"Understood."

"Rainy, you can help me later today. I'll be working the Flying Swings, so you can stay out of sight in the dog house."

"You have a dog?"

"As you have seen, we take in all kinds of strays," she laughed. "And yes, there are several mutts that travel with the carnival, but the dog house is what we call the booth where the ride jocks sit as they control the amusement rides. You'll learn the lingo, honey."

"How can I help?" Gramps asked.

"Well, sir, the wagon you were assigned is where our piano player used to stay. But he sneaked out in the middle of the night two nights ago after he stole some money. He won't be back. We know you play piano, so can you play in his place tonight at the burlesque show?"

Grandpa and I both looked at each other in puzzlement. "How did you know I play the piano? Have you been to Jukie's?"

"No, us carnies don't wander off the lot too much. It was Primrose who mentioned it."

"Primrose?"

"Yes, she's your friend too, right? She was here this morning. When she brought some cinnamon rolls to Earl, he described the two people who came in last night, so she figured out that it was you and Rainy. I think she was greatly relieved to learn that you're here."

"Why did she mention the piano?"

"Well, she stopped in the office to talk to Jones just as I was showing him the Wanted Notice. The three of us spoke a bit about your situation in private, and she assured us the authorities had made a grave error. She said she met you long ago at a dance place where you play piano. We've been friends for years."

"So she knows Jones too? How can that be?"

"Didn't you know she used to travel with us? She worked in the office."

"No, she never mentioned it!"

"She prefers privacy, I think. Her job keeps her here in Endicott now, but Prim still comes around every chance she can. And on Sundays, she often drops in to accompany Earl to our Sunday gathering, which is kind of a catch-all of whatever we want it to be. She keeps a close watch on him."

"They stayed friends too?"

"Friends? Earl is her brother."

12

CAMOUFLAGE

Melba's wagon was warm and welcoming. It was constructed of wood-paneled metal like mine, and it was decorated in hues so bright that Grandpa reckoned the place could cheer up Sigmund Freud.

"You have a patchwork quilt also," I noted.

"Sewing and other handiwork is a carny tradition. It keeps us out of trouble. Maybe you and Gramps should try it," she teased.

As I sat on a chair in front of a mirror that hung over her small dressing table, I watched her cut off my long hair to a bob that skimmed my face just below my ears. She was quite skilled and managed to cut it evenly. However, I had worn my hair long most of my life, so the girl looking back at me from the mirror was unfamiliar. But the more I looked at the stranger, the more I liked her.

Melba then taught me how to apply lipstick. I had never worn makeup before, but I admired the effect. She was right—it made me look much older. "You look beautiful," she smiled, quite satisfied with her work.

"I agree with Melba, but I've lost my tomboy," Gramps said. "There goes the Jennings Street southpaw."

"You'll adjust to the look," she reassured him. "Now you sit over there by my sink so I can work my magic on you next."

Gramps looked a bit apprehensive, but as he took a seat, he winked at me and said, "Life is an experiment, Rainy. We are in the Observation Stage. Take mental notes."

Within an hour, Gramps was almost unrecognizable. Melba dyed his hair and brows dark brown and shaved off his mustache. She even made his brows thinner, just as she had done for me. I couldn't stop laughing when he flopped around like a beached fish during the plucking treatment. When she was done, I marveled to see how much younger he looked.

"Thank you, Melba. You sure turned me into a handsome devil. I believe I could pass for Cary Grant, don't you, ladies? How much do we owe you?"

"We trade services here, not money. Tonight you can just play my favorite Nat King Cole song for me, 'Mona Lisa.' How does that sound?"

"It's a deal! But it might be hard to perform while fending off all the ladies who can't resist my sharp new look."

Melba and I giggled as he strutted around the wagon and posed in front of the mirror with mock exaggeration.

"I'll get Bugg to protect you from the female frenzy. Now, you head on over to the office behind the cook wagon and find Jones. I think he has some daytime work for you. I'll take this lovely little movie starlet with me and start teaching her the ropes.

———

Everything around me was unfamiliar but very exciting. By daylight, the carnival was a lot seedier than it was under all the nighttime lights. However, it was still magical. "I love the midway!" I told Melba.

"Here on the grounds, we don't call this part the midway. We call it the amusement area because our entire carnival includes only rides, games, and shows, but no animals or displays. We're allowed to come back here every year because we run a pretty fair show. Only a few of our games are tipped."

"Yeah, when I was here with Tommy, I saw the guy who runs the Guess Your Weight Game stepping on the scale when he thought no one was looking."

"Jones would throw him out for that. Fortunately, he's already gone. That was the same guy who played the piano by the bally platform where the girls dance. We're not supposed to take cake either."

"Cake?"

"That's what we call the money that grifters keep when they short-change customers. Once word gets out we're doing something like that, the locals beef to the cops, and then the towns don't let us come back."

"So, everybody here is real honest?"

"No, I ain't exactly saying that. Some grifters are so good they don't get caught. We've got all types here."

"Gramps said some carnivals have ex-cons."

"That's true. I'm sure there are a few, but we don't poke around too much in other people's business. Some workers have jail records because they were locked up just for being a carny. Folks tend to be suspicious of us, especially those of us who don't look like what other people consider normal. Many of us became carnies 'cause we can't get work anywhere else. No one hires people who look like Earl or Sim or Viv ... or like me, for that matter. And without work, we don't have a place to live and no way to get by."

"But aren't you embarrassed when people stare?"

"We're all used to it. All our lives, people have stared. At least here we're with others who are equally shunned by 'polite society,' which is one of the most contradictory terms you will ever hear."

"Do the carnival workers who don't have physical problems ever say cruel things?"

"No. And Jones would fire them if they did. But other carnies know better. Most of them understand the courage it takes just to get through life with a bad physical affliction. That's why we protect each other. We respect each other's oddities. Although we tease each other, we're never cruel. No one makes fun of me, and I'm sure you've noticed that I could pass for a zipper."

I enjoyed Melba's sense of humor. She made the unusual seem normal. And that was exactly what I needed because my life was becoming more bizarre by the hour.

When we finally got to the dog house at the Flying Swings, Melba relieved a man named Porter who had been running the ride for her, as they were all trained to cover for each other from time to time.

Melba showed me how to operate the levers inside. It was fairly easy, but she ran the ride a few times as a demonstration. If a swing started spinning erratically, that was a sign of a potential equipment failure, indicating it was time to shut down the ride for further inspection. Also, any grinding sounds or sparks were definite reasons for alarm.

I learned that intermittent power failure was a frequent challenge, especially at night when all the lights were powered up. When that happened, the tickets were returned, and everyone was assured that when the ride was operable again, they would be treated to an extra-long ride.

As we watched the swings go around, Melba told me to look out for people who were sick or for anyone toying with the seat belts. "I've seen people unlatch the safety straps, and I've caught a few idiots trying to stand up."

"While the swings are moving?"

"Yes. There is always someone drunk enough that they are willing to show off on a dare. We have seen people pull dumb stunts on all the rides. One guy even tried to switch seats on a moving roller coaster! If someone attempts to do something prohibited, they are banned from the rides forever. Of course, we can't always remember their faces, but if Jones is around, he takes a photograph of them. People like that are big liabilities for the show."

As soon as the ride was over, Melba then showed me how she called in a crowd. Of course, the show wasn't open yet, but she pretended there were folks gathered and acted out how she welcomed each person as she collected the tickets and encouraged more people to line up. Her act was not only impressive but also very amusing.

Melba promised her audience they could swing around until "their guts flew out" and still have a good time. "Best high you can get without being drunk," she yelled as she spoke to her imaginary visitors. She loved rhymes and shouted:

"Where you going, little Lizzy,
'you afraid of gettin' dizzy?

Hey big fella in the hat
'you a little 'fraidy cat?"

I could tell that she enjoyed teaching me. "The one thing to remember, Rainy, is to be gracious at all times, but try to keep them from walking away."

"You're a good barker, Melba."

"We call that a "talker" because talkers chat up the

customers to stir up maximum enthusiasm. Our best talkers are the ones on the bally stage who rev up the audience for the burlesque show and the freak show. They yell till their voices get sore, but they are a show all by themselves. They use humor to keep the crowd entertained while they wait for more people to gather. It's a real talent. My husband used to be a talker for the freak show."

"Your husband?"

"Yes, he was a human anomaly like me. He was what we call a 'bender.' He could bend his joints backward and forward. You've never seen a better contortionist. But his condition was caused by a soft-bone disease. The fancy name is osteomalacia. It finally killed him at only thirty-five years old. I miss him a lot, but I never feel alone because I have such a big carny family."

I understood why Melba felt that way. I was surrounded by so many new and interesting folks that I didn't have time to think about what was lost. At least, not then.

13

WALNUTS

When we all caught up for dinner that night, Grandpa said Jones had asked him if he could do bookkeeping. He told Gramps that Marny, the lady who had her hand cut off in an accident, had been his right-hand man. "No pun intended with the hand remark."

Gramps had always kept his own landscaping books, so he could do math in his head faster than anybody I knew. When I gave him complicated multiplication and division challenges that involved huge numbers, I was always amazed at his speed and accuracy. He laughed when I told him he would make a great bookie.

It was a relief to know my grandpa was safe inside Jones's trailer, out of sight from almost everyone other than the other carnies. Gramps was grateful to have a few quiet moments to figure out how to resolve our dilemma.

By the time we sat down at the picnic table for a dinner of spaghetti with fist-size meatballs, Vivian was already there. She whistled at Grandpa when we walked up to the table, which made Grandpa blush and sputter a little. His momentary loss of composure was hilarious.

As I was in the middle of twirling a forkful of spaghetti, a woman with a full beard sat down next to me. I was curious why she wore her beard to dinner. Tommy DiGiovanni once told me that bearded ladies attached fake beards with adhesive. She had chosen a long beard, so I couldn't imagine how she was going to keep the nasty-looking thing out of her spaghetti.

The bearded lady introduced herself to Gramps and me with a musical southern drawl. "Howdy. My name's Alva, and I already know who you two are. You're the Fords, and you've been traveling with us for three years since the girl graduated from school. I understand you're from the Trenton, New Jersey area. Now please pass the Parmesan cheese."

That conversation jolted me. The details about us rolled off her tongue effortlessly, as though it were fact. I quickly got the message that not only did we have fake names, but we also had a fabricated history. New Jersey! All I knew about that place was that during the Revolutionary War, George Washington and his Continental Army crossed the Delaware from Pennsylvania and entered New Jersey at McConkey's Ferry. Thankfully, I was paying attention in school during that lesson.

"Where are you from, Alva?" I asked.

"I'm from Louisiana. 'Great place, but I had to leave there because it gets too darn hot for hirsute types like me."

"Hirsute?"

"Hairy." She stroked her beard as though she were petting a puppy. "Viv thinks she's the most beautiful person here, but she knows I'm serious competition," she teased. "Dang, it's warm tonight!"

"Can't you remove your beard to stay cool?"

There was a moment of silence at the table before everyone started laughing. I was bewildered by their response until Alva leaned closer to me and winked conspiratorially. "Oh sugar, I can't take off my beard. This is real. It's an endocrine problem. I have too many male hormones. As a result, I sweat a lot too, but I refer to that as 'dew' or 'evening mist,' depending on the time of day."

I loved how she laughed at herself, and I was fascinated at how they all seemed to accept each other's physical differences. I tried to see past their oddities, but I'd be a world-class liar if I didn't admit that many carnies were shocking in appearance.

My father always taught me to look beyond a person's façade into his soul, but my eyes were taking time to adjust. The carnies were so different from any people I had ever met that in my mind, I was just an observer who had gained free admittance to the "World Renowned Freak Show" that the carnival's flyers promised its guests.

I didn't think of myself as better, but I was tremendously relieved not to be a freak. Many freaks had physical challenges that were so disturbing to imagine living with, that out of fear, I mentally separated myself from them. In my mind, they were the *others*.

After finishing our supper, we followed the routine and scraped our dirty plates before placing them in a stack for washing. Alva cleaned Vivian's plate for her because Vivian was nearly immobile and needed help with almost everything.

There were a lot of able-bodied carnies milling about as well. Gramps said they were the roustabouts, or "rousties" who helped set up and break down the show, maintain the equipment, or act as ride jocks that ran the rides. Some had huge muscles like Bugg, while others were wiry but appeared to be very fit. Several rousties helped lift Vivian from her reinforced bench so she could use her customized wheelchair to return to her quarters. It was nice to see how everyone worked together as a community.

Gramps and I were ready to go back to our wagons when a startling thing occurred. Sim, the young man with only a trunk, suddenly appeared overhead. He was dangling from a cable with only one hand. "Bugg is looking for you," he shouted before swinging in the direction of the amusement rides via the many overhead cables that traversed the grounds.

As I turned around, I saw Bugg heading our way carrying a paper sack. When he reached the eating area, he had to duck to avoid getting caught in the ropes of overhead lighting. He nodded to Gramps and me before handing me the bag.

When I opened it, I saw a shoe. It was the one I had lost near the creek the night before during our attempt to flee from the authorities. The realization hit me that Bugg had risked being caught while sneaking down to the woods to search for my shoe. I was touched, and very grateful.

After I put my shoe on, Bugg then reached into his pocket and handed me some walnuts. "Stain," he mumbled.

Gramps and I started laughing, and Bugg joined in with his strange hee-haw chuckle. I wrapped my arms around him and gave him a big hug. "Thank you for taking such good care of us," I told him.

I could feel our speech-impaired protector breathe with satisfaction as he patted me on the head. "She safe," he said.

14

NIGHT TERRORS

During our first day at the carnival, our eye-opening experiences helped take our minds off our situation for a short while even though we had no solution regarding the trouble we were in. We were just relieved to have a temporary place to hide from anyone who might come looking for us.

Grandpa stayed in the office most of the afternoon, helping the boss with receipt tallies. According to Jones, Officer Montelongo usually came around every night. They were on friendly terms, so Jones promised to get an update on our predicament.

"You are so kind to us," Gramps told the boss. "We're strangers to you, and yet you protect us at your own risk, which is generous and selfless."

Jones shrugged as a way of dismissing Grandpa's praise. "Reese, everybody comes to us as a stranger. And most of us have a sharp sense about who is good and who ain't so good. The bad ones usually don't last too long. We pay attention to how you treat others. As long as you're respectful and non-judgmental, we'll treat you the same way in return. It's obvious that you didn't abduct nobody, so we will fight to help you two stay together. We respect family, and we hate cops."

"We are mighty grateful, Jones."

Gramps and Jones tossed around some ideas about our situation while Gramps added receipts and recorded the financial transactions in thick ledgers. Marny's departure had left the office in upheaval, but Jones quickly realized that Gramps could do more than just record numbers. "You make a good roughey," the boss said, explaining to Gramps that the word meant "management-type helper."

My grandfather was also looking forward to a turn at the piano. However, I was worried about him being more exposed than when he was in the office out of the public eye. "Don't worry honey. I'll be out of sight, and Jones is sending Bugg to stand guard. Right now, I need music. When the notes take flight in my brain, they drown out the useless clatter. That's how I find clarity, and I need that now more than ever."

"Where will we go next, Gramps? Have you got a plan?"

"No, but from now on we need to think before acting, because no good decisions ever come from a place of panic."

"Do you think this just a red tape thing you can get straightened out, or do we have good reason to be frightened?"

"Honey, I don't want you to be alarmed, but this is indeed a serious situation with no easy solution, and I'm afraid my initial decision for us to run only made things worse. My knee-jerk reaction was made out of fear, which was foolish on my part, and I apologize for that. But as a result, we are now at a place where, as Robert Frost would describe it, 'two roads diverge in a yellow wood.' And I need to choose the correct road for us to follow."

"I know in my heart that you're going to figure this out. And I know how much you're sacrificing for me, Gramps.

Thank you." At the time, I had no idea how big his sacrifice would be.

———

It was time for Gramps to play, so we sneaked over to the bally stage, staying far from the amusement section in the areas where no outsiders were allowed. As always, we walked in the shadows until we came to the main stage area. Even though Grandpa now looked significantly different with his dark hair, Jones had given him a pair of clear glasses so he could further disguise himself from anyone who might see him from afar.

The piano was at ground level, but on orders from the boss, Bugg moved it farther to the left of the stage and back into the shadows away from the lights. He arranged it at an angle so when Gramps played, his back was all that would be seen by any passersby.

As Bugg stood vigil by Gramps and me, we communicated with hand signals. I got a big kick out of how the lumbering man moved to the music, snapping his fingers and wiggling his hips. When I started giggling, he exaggerated his movements until we were all laughing uproariously.

Bugg stayed with us until Sim came by to tell him the Ferris wheel gears needed attention. After Bugg rushed off with Sim on his back, I hung out by the piano with Gramps, where I could see and hear everything that was going on.

The talker who was up on the stage trying to rouse a crowd intrigued me. He engaged the audience by teasing them with promises of exciting acts and beautiful girls. He appeared to be very young, perhaps eighteen or nineteen years old, and he was very handsome, which made him perfect as a pitchman. I was amazed at his nonstop patter. As he pranced around the stage, he kept up an interesting and entertaining spiel without missing a beat.

"Gather 'round because you are about to meet three beautiful girls as they shimmy and sparkle like tinsel on a tree," the talker yelled. "Come on up here closer. They call me 'Bear,' but I don't bite, so don't be shy! These mysterious and alluring ladies from the Middle East will perform ancient and exotic dances that will make you dream of Arabian nights. What is under all those veils and chiffon garments, you may ask? Well, those of you who have the great opportunity to go inside the tent will see even more of these lovely creatures than you see out here on this stage tonight."

As a taste of what was to come, three girls paraded across the stage in skimpy costumes, waving to the men in the crowd. One girl had skin the color of almonds while the other two were wearing dark makeup to create a more "exotic" effect. When one dancer draped a chiffon scarf around Bear's neck, he rolled his eyes and pretended to choke while following her around the stage. The audience loved his antics.

Throughout the action, Gramps played whatever music he felt appropriate each time Bear cued him. Sometimes he chose dramatic music to help with the buildup, and other times he chose more lighthearted pieces. For the girls, he played an exotic tune from that old "Arabian Nights" movie.

The pitch was going smoothly until an inebriated audience member jumped up on the stage and started chasing the girls, who screamed and immediately disappeared back behind the curtain. Bear managed to catch the lout and wrestle him to the wood floor. They landed with a resounding thud and then continued tussling. When the drunk's pants slipped down around his knees during the scuffle, the audience cheered wildly.

As soon as the chaos started, Gramps spontaneously

launched into "Turkey in the Straw," eliciting hoots of laughter from the spectators. Bear, happy to see that the audience was still enjoying themselves, shot Gramps a look of appreciation while two rousties ushered the tipsy interloper off the stage.

The ruckus caused more lookie-loos to gather just as Bear was calling a few carnival oddities onto the stage. An Indian "fakir" stuck several long needles into his face, causing a few people in the audience to gasp. Bear promised that anyone who entered the tent would see the Indian fakir lie on a bed of "excruciatingly painful" nails. "We call him Pincushion," he winked, keeping the audience in a playful mood.

After that, a comedian told several jokes before the last performer came out onto the stage to give the folks a taste of magic with a sleight-of-hand act. By then, the crowd had grown even larger and noisier.

Sensing that the energy of the crowd was geared up to a peak, Bear promised bigger thrills for those who would pay fifty cents to enter the tent. With a dramatic flourish, he opened the tent curtain and began to usher the excited attendees inside as Gramps instinctively played the dramatic opening notes of Beethoven's "Symphony No. 5," to everyone's delight.

For that brief interlude, we forgot our troubles and enjoyed feeling like ourselves once again. As the last of the people queued up and the show slowly moved inside the tent, Gramps whispered, "Let's treat them to 'Chopsticks' as a wrap-up number, kiddo." I sat down on the bench next to him, excited to join in, but I never got that chance.

Suddenly a hand emerged from the dark so quickly that we both gasped. Before could turn around, the person squeezed Grandpa's shoulder and whispered, "Reese and Rainy, I've been looking for you."

15

THE YELLOW WOOD

Gramps and I were so startled, we couldn't move. When Grandpa clutched his heart, I was terrified that he might keel over and die. As we both struggled to catch our breath, we turned around slowly and stared up at the person who could barely be seen in the shadows. Finally, Grandpa focused his eyes and stuttered, "Prim-Primrose?" His chest was still heaving.

"Yes, Reese, it's me," she whispered.

I was never so relieved or happy to see anyone in my life, and I could see that Gramps felt the same way. I jumped up to hug her, and she held me close. "Have you come to take us home with you?" I asked.

"I'm trying to help in every way I can, Rainy," she nodded. "I've been looking all over for you two. My brother Earl told me you were playing tonight, Reese. When I first got here, I didn't even recognize you, but I would know your piano playing anywhere."

"Primrose," Grandpa said again, as though that was the only word he could find.

"I didn't mean to startle you, Reese, but I didn't want to speak out and call attention to anything going on over here."

"Thank God, it's you!" he said as his breathing became more steady.

"I'm so happy you're here," I cried.

Primrose kept looking over her shoulder as if worried that she might have been followed. "Let's go somewhere private where we can talk."

Gramps was still so rattled he didn't even bother with his usual routine of closing the lid on the piano and wiping everything off. He gestured for Primrose to follow us as we headed the back way to our wagons.

———

As soon as we got inside my wagon, we locked the door. Grandpa hugged Primrose, and then we all sat down to hear what was going on outside the carnival grounds.

"I see you have Marny's wagon," she said to me. "I heard she left. She always kept it so welcoming and immaculate."

"We were amazed to hear you came by, Prim. We didn't know you had anything to do with the carnival until we were told that Earl is your brother," Gramps said.

"Yes, and that's how I learned you were here. When I came to visit him, he reported that a local man had arrived one night with his granddaughter. He was so moved that you were not too repulsed to shake his hand, Reese. Earl recounted the details in French so no one else would understand us."

"You and Earl speak French? That's almost as impressive as my ability to speak pig Latin," I joked.

Prim's rumbling laugh was as joyful as a night at Jukie's. "Yes, Rainy. My father grew up in France. French is one of three languages Earl can read and speak whenever he does try to talk. He used to speak clearly, but nowadays, he usually converses only with me because few people can make out what he's saying, so he prefers silence.

"I've noticed that he finds other ways to speak, though. He and Bugg make sounds they each understand," I said.

"When people can't speak, Rainy, they learn to be better listeners," Gramps interjected.

"Your Grandfather is right. But Earl prefers isolation more than he did when he was younger. This is the only place that's safe for him. On the outside, he was taunted so much it was unbearable."

"I admire him. A person would have to be strong to live with such physical challenges," Grandpa said.

"Yes, Earl is very brave. He was born with neurofibromatosis, a disease that causes fibrous growths. He was only sixteen when our parents were killed in a boating accident. I was barely eighteen, so there was no way I could care for him, and I didn't want to put him in an institution, especially because he's so bright and talented. That's when we found a home with Jones's show."

"How did Earl feel about that?"

"He was relieved. Jones had posted a local ad looking for a graphic artist, so he hired my brother for his talent, not for the freak show. And he has always treated him well. He's not like some of the other carnival owners who treat people like Earl abominably."

"Jones has certainly been good to Gramps and me."

"He's a quirky little fellow, but I adore him. Every time they set up in towns that are driving distance from Endicott, I come to see them all. When Earl told me you were here, I was so relieved. I've been working to straighten out this ridiculous bureaucratic mess you're in."

"You have?"

"Of course I have. Don't you know how much I care about you two?"

"Yes, I believe I do. But I was afraid we would never see you again," Grandpa said. "I planned to send word once we found a direction."

"I was worried myself. But because of my position as secretary for our city councilman, I had access to the paperwork snafu surrounding your legal relationship with Rainy. I also enlisted everyone at Jukie's to sign a petition objecting to the ridiculous court ruling that claims you're not Rainy's legal guardian."

"I don't understand why we need a piece of paper to tell me who my grandfather is! What they're doing is not right!"

"No, it's not, but I need some time, Rainy. I told Councilman Anthony the entire story, so he's writing letters to all the local newspapers in hopes a reporter will take up your cause. Of course, I haven't told him where you are."

Grandpa rubbed his forehead with his hand and sighed. "I can't tell you how much we appreciate your efforts, but there's so much bureaucracy to deal with. Do you think letters will work, Prim?"

"I don't know, but I have a fallback plan. I'm researching to see if you can adopt your late son posthumously. Then you would be Rainy's legal grandfather."

"Is that even possible?"

"Who knows? But I intend to find out. If nothing else, such a radical idea might garner some attention, so we might get someone with influence to take up your cause."

"Primrose, I can't let you-"

"You can't stop me," she said, cutting him off. "I've never forgotten how you gave me money last year after I broke my leg and was out of work for three months. You wouldn't even let me pay it back. It's now my chance to turn over every rock for you, Reese, so let's fight the bureaucrats together."

"Are they all crazy or just evil?" I asked.

Primrose shook her head in disgust. "Unfortunately, there are some do-gooders who think they're protecting you, Rainy, and I suppose there are always a few lawyers and politicians who are just trying to make a name for themselves."

"Imagine being accused of abducting your own granddaughter! Losing Rainy would be the end of me," Gramps said sadly.

"I will fight them to the end, Reese, but for now, you need to stay out of sight."

"Unfortunately, we didn't plan for this, so we don't have anywhere to go."

"Earl and I inherited our family home near Mount Pleasant, Pennsylvania. It's modest, but I have maintained it over the years in case Earl ever wants to return. You and Rainy can stay there while I try to straighten this out for you. Our friends at Jukie's are helping me, so hopefully you won't have to be there very long."

"I just don't know what to say, Primrose. I worry about you getting involved in something that could bring you trouble."

Prim dismissed his comment with a wave of her hand. "I'm a colored woman, remember? I'm familiar with trouble. It doesn't scare me. It motivates me. Please let me help you and Rainy."

"All right, my dear. But if we get caught, the consequences could be dire."

"I hate to remind you, but your situation is already dire."

16

TACTICAL PAUSE

In history class, I learned that in battle, sometimes the commander will order a tactical pause for the troops to regroup before advancing. Gramps and I knew we were in the middle of a tough battle, but we also needed time to plan.

The following day, Primrose came to visit us after she spent time with Earl. Gramps was different when Prim was around. Despite our situation, he seemed relaxed and content to be in her presence. I loved the way he looked at her, and I also loved the way she cared for us.

We were amazed when she told us that although her brother could not control his throat and misshapen mouth when speaking, he could do so while singing. According to Prim, he could sing with a voice that was not only beautiful but also articulate. However, I didn't know if we would be with the carnival long enough to hear him perform. Our priority was to figure out an exit plan.

After much debate, it was decided that the wisest thing to do was to hole up at the carnival for two more weeks until the show jumped to its new location.

Prim explained that during relocation when the rousties are packing up the dismantled rides and games, there's a lot of hectic activity. Wagons, mobile concession stands, trailers, and trucks loaded with equipment move out at various times all day long, allowing for opportunities for us to slip out without being noticed. She also assured us we would be safe on carnival grounds for the next two weeks. "Oh, and incidentally, I located a car so that once you get out of town to someplace safe, you'll have transportation."

"How did you get a car?"

"Our mutual friend Millie Mae had a Pontiac that has been sitting in the driveway since she passed on. I'm also friends with her daughter Pearl, who agreed to let me take it with no questions asked. So in two weeks, you can move on from here if the councilman and I haven't made headway regarding your case."

"You've done so much for us, Prim. I don't know how we will ever be able to repay you."

"Reese, you have already given so much to me, and you've helped so many of our friends. Everyone at Jukie's knows you constantly checked in on Indian John Joe to make sure he had groceries, and you visited Millie Mae almost every day during those last few months of her life. You never mentioned those things to anyone, but we always knew. John Joe once told me, 'Reese don't see us in colors, he just brings the color.' That crazy old renegade said it best for all of us."

Gramps looked a little embarrassed, but I could tell her words meant a lot to him. They meant a lot to me too. All my life I have known that Grandpa is one of the kindest people in the world, but he never took credit for all the things he did for others. It was just his nature. My dad was the same way. He just wasn't here long enough to become a grandfather himself.

"That's kind of you, Primrose," Gramps said. "I hope I can

get back to Jukie's one day soon. In the meantime, we will wait out our time in Pennsylvania while you see what you can do about straightening out the paperwork. Hopefully, that won't take more than a few weeks."

"We just need to get you and Rainy out of here first, Reese. Sooner or later, the cops are going to show up with a warrant."

"We need to buy some time"

"Yes, and you should be safe here a while longer, but when the time comes, you and Rainy will need to slip out in one of the vans, and I'll bring Millie Mae's old car around to a prede-termined place outside of town where I will meet up with the van. But I must caution you that with almost every move, locals hang around the exits to watch the freaks as they leave. For them, it's like a free show. Despite your new look, some of your neighbors might recognize you, so it's imperative that you not be seen. Our timing must be precise."

———

It's very stressful to know you are being pursued like a criminal. Gramps and I were constantly looking over our shoulders, and although we felt safe with the carnies, every afternoon when the carnival opened, we had to disappear into the background.

Several times when the rousties addressed me as "Miss Ford," I didn't acknowledge them. I found it very hard to adapt to a new name so quickly. Each day, I had to remind myself that our situation was temporary and that it would all be resolved soon.

Bugg watched over Gramps and me all the time. Jones even had Bugg's trailer moved right next to our wagons so he would be there all the time when he wasn't working. And during the day, when he was working, he took me with him.

I caught on to the work routine very quickly. Every morning, starting very early, the rousties hustled around checking the mechanisms on all the rides to make sure everything was operable. Reno was up before sunrise preparing food in the cookhouse while the carnies who worked the concessions loaded in their food supplies to get ready for the day.

Gramps got an early start too. He was determined to help Jones get his books in order during our brief stay, so after we had breakfast together, he and Jones went off to the office. At each meal, we met new people who were on varying schedules, so each meal was a social occasion.

Bear, the talker who had emceed the bally show, showed up at breakfast bleary-eyed and exhausted. After Jones introduced us, Bear didn't chat long. He apologized for not being social, explaining how every morning he woke up with a sore throat, so he usually kept chatter to a minimum. That came as no surprise to me after witnessing his exuberant performance the night before.

He did linger long enough to thank Gramps for an outstanding performance. "Your musical choices made chaos seem like part of the act. Thank you so much for that." He smiled at me and then took a seat by himself. I noticed that no one else sat next to him, as the other carnies seemed to know and honor his routine of solitude.

After breakfast, Melba met up with Bugg and me so we could help prep the rides for the new day. Although Bugg could hardly speak, he had his own language. The secret was to pay attention to all the various ways he communicated without words.

While Bugg was a "floater" who worked on rides that needed his expertise, Melba was assigned to the Ferris wheel. She washed the seats with warm water, and then I helped by drying the vinyl with a soft cloth.

I was surprised to see how dirty the cars were after the previous day of activity. We had to scrape gum and dried food off the seats, seatbelts, and the safety bars that came down to hold people inside the cars. There was a rainbow of food colors, from red ketchup and yellow mustard to bright blue cotton candy.

One seat even had excrement on it. "We should have expected this," she grinned, pointing to the number on the side of the car. "This is car number two!" We both had a great laugh about that.

We scrubbed and cleaned each seat so they looked like new again, although several were damaged. A guy named 'Spike" had carved his name on one seatback, and there were a few cigarette burns as well. Melba explained that every year there were losses because of damage.

The good part of our job was that we found a lot of money that had fallen out of loose pockets during the rides. On one seat, we found a money clip full of bills. "This is so exciting," I said. "It's like finding hidden treasure."

"It is fun," Melba laughed. "But we're on the honor system. We usually put all the money we find into a kitty to go toward repairing some of the damage, but not everyone is trustworthy. We have a few dishonest people here, but I think most try to be honest."

As we continued to follow Bugg around and work the rides, we found other treasures. When Bugg brought over a beautiful scarf he untangled from one of the Flying Swings, I stroked the silken fabric with admiration. The sunset colors reminded me of a Georgia O'Keeffe painting I had seen in one of my father's many art books.

"You keep that scarf, Rainy," Melba said. "We pool the money, but we can keep articles of clothing and such if we find something we can use. You go on and take it now. It's yours."

She tied the scarf around my neck and then stepped back to admire the effect. "It looks beautiful on you."

"It sure does!" I reeled around to see Bear, who was walking past us toward his trailer. He nodded and let out a long wolf whistle. "Beautiful!"

Suddenly, my cheeks were blistering hot. I would have hidden behind Melba, but that would have been as effective as hiding behind a garden hose. However, a part of me secretly loved Bear's attention. Although I had not had much experience with boys, I certainly noticed them. And no one could miss Bear.

"That kid is too good-looking and self-confident for his own good," Melba laughed. "But we all love him."

All I managed to say was, "Uh-huh," which made Melba laugh even more.

Bugg, who was watching the entire incident, mumbled, "Pretty miss."

I knew I wasn't unattractive, but I had never thought of myself as beautiful. I was a tall and slender tomboy, and according to Tommy, I was nothing more than a clumsy giraffe with a great pitching arm. Grandpa's friends at Jukie's often commented on my deep blue eyes and white-blonde hair, and my teacher once commented that I had perfect teeth, but that's just what nice people do. I knew I was no Grace Kelly, but it sure was special when Bear whistled at me.

"What else can we clean?" I asked with exaggerated nonchalance while trying to hide my smile.

However, the moment I bent over to collect a few pieces of trash, my warm feeling was immediately replaced with an onslaught of anxiety. There at my feet was another flyer with a picture of me and Gramps on it. I was abruptly reminded of why we were running, and I panicked.

I yanked at the scarf around my neck because I couldn't get

my breath. I was convinced I was suffocating. I pulled at my hair and clutched my throat. I was sure I was going to die.

Out of nowhere, Bugg produced a paper bag, tightened it around my nose and mouth, and then ordered me to breathe. I felt safe with Bugg, so I did as I was told. As I breathed into the bag, I detected the smell of corndogs, so I knew Bugg had retrieved the bag from the trash, but I kept on inhaling. Finally, my chest stopped heaving.

As soon as Melba saw that I was calm again, she picked up the paper and crumpled it. "They are looking for a girl named Lorraine Merrill. Your name is Rainy Ford. You're with us, and you are safe. Don't you forget that!"

17

CONNECTIONS

I helped Melba and Bugg every day before the gates opened. After we cleaned the rides, Melba and Bugg tested them multiple times to make sure the gears were operable. Once they were satisfied that the equipment was running smoothly, they let me ride. Being alone on the rides was thrilling, and during the occasional moments when I was able to suppress my anxiety, I felt like I was on a magical vacation. Big Eli was my favorite amusement ride because I was high above the world where I was safe and untouchable. But as soon as my feet hit the ground, I had to fight the urge to run.

In the evening, Gramps was always in my wagon so he could help Bugg keep watch over me. Although the carnies were always milling about and the atmosphere was festive, Gramps worried constantly, so I understood why he needed to stay close.

Melba often dropped in to check on me too. We found it humorous that every time she showed up, she was chewing on something. Although she was the thinnest person I had ever seen, she ate constantly to strengthen her bones to prevent them from breaking so easily. She told us that one of her arms had shattered eight times!

I knew her gums were deteriorating, but it was shocking to see her spit out a tooth while chewing on a slice of orange. However, Melba had a great sense of humor about her physique and referred to herself as Olive Oyl, the character in the comic strip "Popeye." She joked that her skeletal physique was an asset because she never had to worry about being trapped in her wagon, as she could always slip out under the door.

One time Melba brought a carny with her whom we had not yet met. "Reese and Rainy, meet my best friend," she said by way of introduction. "She's billed as 'Sonia Saber,' but you can just call her Esther. We've worked together for years."

Esther shook everyone's hand. "I'm pleased to meet you all. We love having new folks around, although I understand that you have been with the show for three years," she winked.

Esther was captivating. She had black hair and blue-violet eyes that reminded me of Elizabeth Taylor. She didn't seem to be the type of person to be traveling with a carnival. Esther was so elegant that I envisioned her in a Cadillac on a palm tree-lined street in Hollywood ... or perhaps draped on a lounge while being fed grapes by a Roman gladiator.

"You swallow swords? That's a good trick," I said, unable to disguise my awe.

"We like to think of it more as a skill, Rainy."

"Those are retractable blades on the knives, right?"

"I'm not sure where you heard that, dear."

"Probably from Tommy DiGiovanni," Gramps snickered.

"Yes, he said it's all an illusion."

"Some tricks are, but not sword swallowing. It takes a lot of practice to control the epiglottis and esophageal sphincters that control the natural choking mechanisms in the throat."

"That sounds so dangerous! How do you learn to do that without getting injured?"

"When first learning, we use small knives before working up to the bigger blades. Sword performers have to align the sword so that it goes straight down to the stomach. That's why you see us move our bodies into very controlled positions."

"Do use fake knives made of rubber?"

My question made her giggle. "Even though I don't know that Tommy DiGiovanni boy you mentioned, I suspect that's another one of his suppositions, right?"

"Yeah. He's famous for his encyclopedic catalog of misinformation," I laughed.

"Well, you can inform young Mr. Britannica that we do use metal knives, but they have dull blades; and as I said, working with swords requires training. Although the blades aren't sharp, if a person does it incorrectly, they could sustain a serious or even fatal injury. It happens often. During a sword act, the talker has to keep everybody back. There can be no sudden movements."

"Esther is very talented," Melba said. "She does true performance art with dance moves, music, and ballet movement. I can't wait for you to see her perform."

"What led you to your interest in sword swallowing?" Grandpa asked.

"I'm from Germany, and my parents worked in the circus, which is a highly respected means of employment in Europe. Of course, circuses differ from carnivals, not only because of the animal acts but also due to the stationary locations. Also, instead of featuring an amusement area as the hub, a circus is centered beneath a huge tent known as The Big Top, the place where the main acts are performed. Our location was just outside the beautiful city of Munich."

"So you speak German?" I asked.

"Oh, yes, that is my native language, but I also speak Spanish, French, and Portuguese. I learned from my parents. My father was a very well-known ringmaster, and my mother was an acrobat who could do show-stopping stunts atop horses. When I was young, I wanted to learn a skill so I could participate in the show. One of my mother's good friends was a sword swallower and a fire eater, she taught me those skills."

"You can eat fire, too?"

"Yes, but I prefer not to do it. To tell you the truth, fire terrifies me. One circus fire is all it takes to make one never want to see a flame again. I don't even like candles," she laughed.

"What an interesting life!" Grandpa exclaimed. "So what brought you here?"

"My father was a Jew, and when Hitler was coming into power, we could feel the winds of change in Germany and all over Europe, so he decided it was time to leave. My parents relocated to Norway, and during that time, I was hired to do a minor role in a film, which brought me to America."

"You were in a movie?"

"Nothing memorable, Rainy. I was offered a few other acting roles, but I missed circus life, which was all I had ever known. My parents passed away just before the war broke out, so I remained here and sought employment with a carnival. I've been with this show ever since, and I have made so many wonderful friends. I understand you know my other dear friend, Primrose."

"Oh my goodness, you know Primrose too?" Gramps exclaimed.

"Of course, she's been coming around for years to take care of her brother, Earl."

"Of course, it makes sense that would know her too, but I'm still stunned"

"Because we're all friends?" Melba asked.

"That is certainly a pleasant surprise. But what amazes me most is that amid our recent and nerve-wracking turn of events, I somehow forgot what a small, but beautiful world this is."

18

MAPLES

The following day was a Sunday, and I was excited to hear Easy Earl sing. Gramps and I were going to attend the gathering with Melba, Esther, Jones, Bugg, and Prim. Gramps and I loved being part of such an interesting group. Despite knowing them only a short time, they seemed like longtime friends. Gramps referred to it as "foxhole friendship," because it doesn't take long to grow close to those who have your back when the enemy is closing in.

Although I was anticipating Earl's performance, I couldn't imagine how he could sing while not being able to articulate words well enough to speak. It was apparent that the immense growth on his neck impeded his breathing, causing him to pant between bites of food when eating.

"How do you think he does it?" I asked my grandfather.

Gramps had a theory. "Two years ago, just before I moved in with you and your dad, I was visiting my old war buddy in Florida when he introduced me to his young neighbor. The kid was only sixteen, but he had just won a local contest for playing guitar and singing. It was a truly remarkable accomplishment because the boy couldn't speak without stuttering. And I must say, it was an extreme stutter—so bad that when he couldn't get through a sentence, he would sing it. I still remember his name was Mel Tillis. I was amazed at how he used another part of his brain to override the part that was tripping him up. I don't know if there's a name for it or not, but I suppose that's what Earl must do. Somehow he has found a way to regulate his throat spasms and breathing so he can sing to express himself."

I was contemplating Grandpa's explanation when Primrose arrived early, long before the gathering. She said she had to help groom Earl so he wouldn't be too shy to perform. I wasn't sure what she meant until she confided in us that Earl's needs were becoming more challenging.

Earl had growths all over his body. He could reach underneath the protrusions on his front side and on his privates to clean them, but he couldn't manage the ones on his backside. Prim explained that if he didn't clean the growths on his back properly, bacteria would collect, causing a smell or a rash or even worse. She was very concerned because the show would be moving on soon, and she hadn't found a full-time assistant to take care of him.

"Wouldn't someone here want to help out for extra money?" I asked.

"Rainy, despite acceptance of their deformities, carnies often have the same reactions you and I have. Everybody loves Earl, but his condition is off-putting, and most people don't want to touch him. I've even seen his nurses and doctors react the same way. Since childhood, he has had endless surgeries and subsequent pain, but the fibroids keep growing, so he has finally given up. Now the condition is threatening his health. There's so much to clean on his back that I'm not even sure I can get it all done in time."

"I can help you if think he would let me."

"Oh, sweetheart, thank you, but I couldn't allow that. His growths are very unpleasant, and I wouldn't want you to have negative feelings about my brother, which would be a natural response. It's better to just like him from afar."

"Primrose, to tell you the truth, when I first met him, I thought his condition was shocking. I tried not to look at him at all, but then when Gramps shook his hand, I imagined it must have been a bit like holding bark in your hand. Now, when I see him at breakfast, I just think of him as a strong tree. I hope that's not insulting. But I'm not afraid to touch him if you need help."

"Reese, what do you think?" she asked.

"If Rainy is willing to assist Earl, why don't you give her a try, Primrose? You help us, so allow us to help you."

———

Although I volunteered to assist Primrose, I was apprehensive about going to Earl's wagon with her, but after she checked with him, she said he was grateful for the offer to help. Earl was accustomed to the reactions of others to his condition, so he was not fearful of how I might respond. However, I was.

When we entered his wagon, I immediately felt at home. He was sitting in a large chair near the window. There were bookshelves everywhere, even more than I had, and there were stacks of books on the floor as well. The walls were painted the same dusty-rose tone I had recently used to paint the interior of my wagon, which I chose because it reminded me of Jukie's. Earl's wagon was equally as inviting.

On one table, there was a collection of model airplanes of all sizes and types, as well as a cluster of glass bottles with ships inside. "Surely you didn't make those," I remarked. As soon as I said it, I feared I had insulted him, but Earl's hands were misshapen and awkward, so to create something so beautiful seemed like an impossible task.

Primrose did not speak up to answer for him. I suspected she was waiting for us to find our own form of communication, just as I had done with Bugg.

Earl reached into a bag on the chair next to him and extracted a long pair of tweezers. He then demonstrated how he could pick up small things by using tweezers, even though his fingers had lost definition because of the thick scales that covered them. His mouth, distorted by grotesque growths, made movements that suggested he was trying to communicate; and after an extended effort, his lips finally released one word. "Delicate," was all he managed to say.

"I understand. I'm too clumsy to do what you do. That's a wonderful tool you have."

"He named it 'Claw,'" Prim smiled.

"Claw, huh? Earl, that thing sure seems handy to me. I would love to watch you put a ship together. I've never seen how ships in a bottle are made, so I would like to learn the process."

While I was examining the ships, Primrose brought over a large basin of warm water. "You know this takes a lot of time, my dear," she said to Earl, "so we need to move quickly to get you to your concert in time." She gestured to Earl to lean forward as she gently removed his shirt.

I had mentally prepared myself not to react negatively when I saw his body, but I was surprised to discover that I was not in the least bit repulsed when I saw him without his shirt. I had already seen his face and neck, which were unlike anything I had ever seen before, but I had adjusted to his deformities, so his body was just more of the same. It might have been even more jarring if his body did not match the rest of him. My eyes were learning to see the world around me in a whole new way.

At first, I was afraid to touch Earl because I didn't want to hurt him, so I closely observed everything Prim was doing. She poured lavender scent into the water before opening a fresh bar of oatmeal soup. With great care, she then washed the largest fibroid on his back, lifting it so she could wipe the undersurface clean. I picked up a facecloth and followed suit. When I lifted a tumor near his spine, I detected an unpleasant odor.

"Oh, I'm sorry!" Primrose said. "That one is offensive."

"No more than Tommy DiGiovanni's feet when he takes off his sneakers," I said. My offhand comment made Prim giggle so much she had to wipe tears from her eyes. I could tell Earl was laughing too, because his shoulders were heaving up and down.

"I don't know who this Tommy kid is, but someday I'm going to have to meet him!" Earl shook his head in agreement, and I felt his body relax more.

It took a long time to wash Earl's torso because we had to make sure each fibroid was dry underneath before we powdered it and allowed it to fall back against his skin. "It's most important not to let moisture get trapped anywhere," Primrose cautioned. "We don't want Tommy's sneakers living up under any of 'em." With that, we all laughed again as though there was nothing unusual about our task.

I found it very relaxing to cleanse and tend to another person, which surprised me. It was especially rewarding to see how much it soothed Earl.

"Will you be singing too?" I asked Prim after Earl shuffled into the bathroom.

"No. Singing is Earl's special talent, and I want the focus to be on him."

"But I love to hear you sing too."

"That's sweet of you to say, Rainy, but I can sing anywhere, and this place is his home, so it's very personal to him. I used to sing duets with him, but he is better as a soloist because he has to work so hard to control his breath. Besides, I relish the opportunity to just sit and listen to his lovely voice."

As Earl reentered the room, he noticed me studying his book collection. I was assessing his interests because I wanted to lend him something from the collection in my wagon. He had a large assortment of books about engineering and medicine, and many others about animals, nature, and even cooking.

When Earl saw me glance up at a framed photo on the bookshelf, he reached past me with the claw and deftly retrieved it for me to examine. The girl in the photo looked to be somewhere around ten years old, but I instantly knew it was Primrose. She was holding the hand of a very handsome and very normal-looking younger boy. "I'm guessing that's you," I smiled.

Earl nodded, and then he held up his hands in a pose to indicate that he had been a beautiful child.

"I agree you were darn cute," I said. "You were just a little sapling in this photo, but look at you now with all your knowledge and skills. You've grown into a mighty maple tree! Maples don't talk either, but the leaves are more beautiful than all the others."

When I noticed tears accumulating around the mound of excess flesh that blocked most of Earl's eye, I was fearful I had somehow embarrassed him or hurt his feelings. Primrose, who saw the concerned expression on my face whispered, "He's fine, Rainy. His tears are good tears ... love drops."

19

DISRUPTION

After donning large sunglasses and a baseball cap to cover my hair, I rushed over to the bally platform where I knew Gramps would be waiting. He, too, was disguised in glasses and a fedora hat. It was our first time to venture away from the back lot in the daytime. The carnival wasn't scheduled to open until noon, so no locals would be about, but we couldn't take any chances.

Jones had invited my grandfather to play piano during the setup as a cheerful prelude to the gathering, and Gramps was more than happy to do so. He was just finishing a lively version of "Twelfth Street Rag" when he saw me. As soon as he wrapped up, he joined me for coffee.

The area was buzzing more than an apiary as rousties arranged seating in front of the platform. Behind the rows of folding chairs, a table had been set up to hold the coffee service. To my delight, Reno was walking around offering everyone his freshly made "elephant ears." The warm, deep-fried dough dusted with powdered sugar and cinnamon was like a birthday party in my mouth.

"Wow! This a decadent confection!" Gramps smiled as he wiped the powdered sugar off his face. "Where have you been all my life, you heart-stopping temptress?" he asked, addressing his half-eaten pastry.

It was a balmy summer Sunday, the kind of day when I would normally be wading in the creek or swinging on a rope as far out over the water as I could--one of those dandelion-puffs-in-the-breeze June days when life is full of promise. Even though I missed my friends, as our new acquaintances gathered around us, I couldn't imagine any activity much more enjoyable.

While waiting for the service to begin, I noticed a few carnies I had not yet met who were taking seats. One man named Winston Hamilton was so tall he looked like an extension ladder. There was also a man with long hair all over his face and body who had no visible skin. I had read about both of them in the billing for the Freak Show, but it was still startling to see them in person rather than as part of a performance. Alongside them sat Esther, Voluptuous Vivian, and several other carnies whose bodies had been altered by nature or happenstance.

I wondered what it was like to be on display as an oddity, and I marveled at how the carnies had formed a community where the "freaks" could display their uniqueness without thinking of themselves as aberrations. No one else appeared to notice them except to wish them a good morning. I felt as though I were a character in a book living in a fictional, upside-down world.

As soon as most of the carnival workers were present, Jones jumped up on the platform and gestured for everyone to quiet down. When the audience settled, Bear stepped out from behind the bally curtain and flashed a dazzling smile. He was wearing a suit and tie, which was very impressive. I was sure I had never seen anyone quite so handsome, except in those teen idol magazines ... and maybe not even in one of those.

After he welcomed everyone, he thanked Jones for hosting and Reno for providing the refreshments. I was surprised when Bear introduced Melba because she was sitting in the audience right next to me.

Rising from her chair, Melba expertly recited the poem, "Hope" by Emily Dickinson. Her delivery was very eloquent. I didn't know much about poetry, but the words touched me. After a round of applause for Melba, Alva, the female carny with a beard, recited 1st Corinthians 1-13, which I remembered from Bible School.

Several other carnies spontaneously shared words or thoughts before Bear introduced Earl. The audience sat in anticipation while we waited for the main act to begin.

As soon as Earl emerged from behind the curtain, everyone cheered. Bear moved to the side of the stage and turned on a tape recorder. When the first few notes of the instrumental version of "Ave Maria" began, Earl stepped farther forward.

At first, he struggled to open his mouth, which was hidden behind a cluster of growths. After a few moments of hesitation and mouth contortions, Earl's tender voice burst forth with clarity and resonance. His tenor range was glorious, and his passion revealed the soul of the man behind the mass of disfiguring growths.

Gramps and I stared at each other in amazement. I turned to Primrose, who was sitting behind me with Bugg. "He's astounding!" I whispered. Prim was glowing with pride.

When Earl's voice trailed off on the ending notes of the song, we all jumped up to give him a standing ovation. Earl remained on stage while Bear pulled a chair over and placed it next to him.

The performance became even more exciting when, seemingly out of nowhere, Sim swung by his arms along the façade of the bally stage and then dropped down onto the chair next to Earl. Once again, Bear started the recorder.

We were all enthralled when the duo launched into "Old Man River," the passionate song by Jerome Kern and Oscar Hammerstein. By the time they got to the "tired of living and feared of dying" lyric, many of the carnies were visibly moved. When Earl and Sim finished the last line about how "ol' man river keeps rolling along," Jones loudly blew his nose as several others in the audience wiped their eyes. Gramps and I were just as affected as all the others.

Rather than end the gathering on a quiet note, there was one more performance scheduled. To my surprise, Bear joined Sim and Earl for a rollicking rendition of "When the Saints Come Marching In." His voice was lower than the others, so they created a marvelous harmony.

The tune was so uplifting that everyone jumped up to clap and sing along. Gramps said he hadn't seen that kind of enthusiastic participation since he attended a Mardi Gras in New Orleans one February long ago. The event was so marvelous I didn't want it to end.

After Bear said a few closing words, everyone in attendance remained quite animated. We were all collecting the folding chairs when Bugg suddenly whistled, bringing the talking and activity to an abrupt halt.

When we looked at Bugg, he gestured toward the front entry gates where the daytime sky was filled with flashing red lights. Everyone stood still as we tried to determine what was happening.

There was a long silence, and then Jones mumbled, "Heads up, everyone. We've got trouble."

———

Melba immediately grabbed Gramps and me by our arms and dragged us to the stage. She lifted the bally cloth, shoved us underneath the stage, and pressed her finger against her lips as a signal for us to remain silent. I was terrified.

We stayed under the stage for a long time, not knowing when it was safe to come out. Eventually, we heard voices approaching the stage. I was shaking so hard Gramps had to put his arms around me to keep me calm.

When the footsteps got closer, I recognized several voices. It was Jones and Primrose, and they were talking to Officer Montelongo.

"As you can see," Jones said, "this is where we have our Sunday performance. I told everyone to wait here, so feel free to take a look around at all these folks. There are no strangers in this crowd. Us carnies don't trust outsiders any more than they trust us, so I'm not sure where you're getting your information from, Officer."

"I'm not accusing you of lying, Jones, but they could be hiding somewhere on the grounds. One of the local teenagers who snuck in under the fence reported seeing a girl out on the back lot who matched the granddaughter's description."

"Maybe you should be after the alarmist little punk who snuck in without paying."

"Tony Montelongo," Primrose interrupted in an oddly cheerful tone, "how long have we known each other? You are well aware that I come around to see my brother every time the carnival is in town, so I am familiar with every carny here at the show. And I can promise you that no one is stupid enough to risk having the show permits revoked by getting involved with local police business."

"I hope not, Primrose, because they'd be harboring fugitives."

"Fugitives? Tony, that's a harsh word. You know this is all a big red tape snafu. Reese Merrill did not kidnap the young lady. She is his granddaughter."

"Primrose is right. The whole matter is utterly ridiculous," Jones grumbled.

"I agree it's a rotten kettle of fish, Jones, but I'm just following orders," Montelongo replied. "I've met the family, and I saw him with the girl at Jukie's dance hall, so I know he's not a common kidnapper. I've also been informed that the gentleman recently suffered a personal loss, which is a darn shame. However, Mr. Merrill needs to straighten out this mess with the court. It's way above my pay grade. In the meantime, I have a job to do."

"Based on a rumor from some teenage punk?"

"The kid who reported the sighting of the girl was sure it was Lorraine Merrill. He said he recognized her from school. How about if you just let me and my partner look around so I can write up a report?"

"You are very welcome to do that, Officer. I'll just need to take a look at your warrant first."

"Really, Jones?"

"Really. To tell you the truth, Montelongo, I'm deeply offended that you barged in unannounced on a Sunday, my day for fasting and worship. A holy day! It's a darn travesty. To make matters worse, it seems you don't have a warrant, so your police business will have to wait until you boys can produce the proper paperwork. In the meantime, you're welcome to sit outside the entrance and keep an eye on us criminals and reprobates if that will make you feel better."

"We were kind of hoping you would help us out so it doesn't have to come to that."

"As I said, you're interfering with my right to worship. I think that's against the law too, isn't it? Didn't I read that as a Civil right somewhere in one of our constitutional amendments? Maybe it was in the Gettysburg Address? Darn, I hate it when I can't remember such things. But I'll bet my lawyer remembers. Maybe I should give him a call."

"Are you threatening--"

"There's no need for conflict, gentlemen," Primrose interrupted. "Let's keep it friendly. Tony, please let me accompany you back to the entrance. We can grab some hot coffee and pastries along the way and you can give me your card so we can contact you if we catch sight of the girl."

Gramps made a move as if he were going to crawl out to turn himself in, but I yanked him back. "Please don't let them take me away," I whispered. I could sense he was even more shaken than I was.

As the footsteps receded, Grandpa and I continued to sit on the dirt under the stage until a firm hand reached under the cloth to grab my arm and pull me out. Bugg had returned with a pull wagon and immediately shoved me into the cart as Jones came around from the back of the stage.

Bugg was throwing a blanket over me when I heard Jones whispering with Gramps. "Wait here until Bugg returns for you."

"We never wanted to bring trouble to your doorstep," Gramps apologized.

"We're used to it. Cops don't like us because we're eccentric. And we hate cops because they're jackasses."

As Bugg wheeled me away, the last I heard Jones say to Gramps was, "They're getting too close. You gotta get outta here before that cop comes back with a warrant and takes away that girl of yours."

20

THE SWERVE

Neither Gramps nor I could sleep that night. We stayed up late with Primrose and Jones to figure out an escape plan.

"We've had a bit of experience with this," Jones reassured us. "We were in Wheeling, West Virginia when a guy came after his wife who had left him to join the show. She didn't want to go with him because he was abusive, but the authorities seemed to think he had a right to take her back like she was a farm animal he had purchased. The husband tried to claim that we kidnapped her, so you can understand why this entire issue has fired my pistons. But our plan to get her out safely worked, so I'm thinking it may work again."

"I remember her well," Prim nodded. "She was a terrific comedian. I was visiting Earl the night you were ready to move out and she slipped away with the show. As I recall, she hid amongst the equipment in one of the vans. Do you think that will work again?"

"Too risky. We have ten days left until we relocate. We can't wait that long. But I can break down a ride that is currently out of operation and start moving it to our next location now. You two can ride in the truck, and then Primrose can meet you with the car once you are far out of town."

"Tomorrow night at dark?" Primrose asked.

We all nodded in agreement.

"Only Bugg will know. No goodbyes to anyone else," Jones told Gramps and me. "We can't afford to have something go wrong."

I couldn't imagine not saying goodbye. "But they are our friends!"

"I know, Rainy. I will have to say your goodbyes for you. They will understand."

That night, when I turned off the light, I was overcome with sadness. I was facing another departure, and I had already experienced the pain of too many endings.

───────

The following day, I skipped work with Melba so I wouldn't accidentally give away our plans. Gramps and I packed our belongings into our pillowcase sacks and hid them under our beds until it was time to go. I carefully folded my chiffon scarf and placed it in my pocket.

We decided it was best to wait till almost everyone had their lunches before we ate. As we were finishing up, Jones came by and slipped a paper envelope under Grandpa's elbow. When Gramps peered inside, he discovered a small pack of bills. "No, Jones, I can't-"

"No protesting allowed," the boss said under his breath. "Do you have any idea how much I would have to pay an accountant to do what you did in lickety-split time? Consider it wages. You'll need it." He walked off, leaving Gramps speechless.

After lunch, we checked on Bugg to see his progress with

packing up the equipment. He was supervising a few other rousties who were breaking down the inoperable Caterpillar ride and hauling the pieces to a truck.

Daylight savings time was still in effect, so we had to wait until after nine o'clock for darkness to set in. Later that evening, according to plan, Bugg whistled as he strolled past our wagons, and then he continued walking. We grabbed our pillowcases and followed him along the darkest part of the back lot to the transport area where all the trucks and larger trailers were parked.

When we got to the moving van, Bugg handed each of us a flashlight so we could crawl in amongst the cars and platform pieces from the ride.

We weren't scheduled to meet Primrose for at least three hours, so Bugg had placed blankets on the seats to make them more comfortable for our journey out of Endicott. I knew there would come a time to feel sad about leaving, but as we rushed into hiding, all I could feel was trepidation.

"You safe," Bugg said. He squeezed my hand and then quickly closed the door of the truck. As it plunged into darkness, Gramps and I switched on our flashlights. While sitting in near darkness, we heard the revving of the engine and the screech of the exit gate when Bugg yanked it open.

It was as simple and as fast as that. We were leaving our place of refuge and the people who had trusted us enough to provide shelter ... and so much more.

————

As the truck slowly moved forward, we heard the gate close again behind us. We had only moved a few yards when suddenly the van came to an abrupt halt.

"What's happening, Gramps?"

"Shh, Rainy. I can't make out what's going on. Just sit tight."

Soon there was a big commotion. Bugg let out his distinctive whistle as if he were calling someone. Within minutes, we heard Jones's voice as it moved closer to our location. He was yelling at someone, but we couldn't make out what he was saying. There was a cacophony of voices and footsteps as people surrounded the truck.

Gramps grabbed my arm. "I think they're onto us, kid. Let's squeeze as far back into the van as we can."

As we climbed over the cars, we heard Jones yelling again. "What the hell do you think you're doing? You can't stop us from moving our equipment!"

"State Police. We're handling this now. We have a warrant," someone answered.

"Let me look at that thing," Jones demanded. After a long pause, he spoke again. "You guys are all a bunch of knuckleheads. This is a warrant to check our lot. Not our truck."

"This is your property, isn't it?"

"Yes, but as you can see, it's outside the lot now, and you have no right to check this any more than you have a right to check my mother's house, and I own that too!"

"You carnies are all alike. Do you carpetbaggers think you can come in and take over our towns and make your own rules? Not in this town. We'll be back tomorrow with a permit to search your trucks. In the meantime, this one isn't going anywhere. "Slash the tires, boys," he ordered.

"You can't do that!" Jones yelled.

"We just did. The truck stays here, and we'll be watching it all night long."

———

I was so frightened I could hardly hold my urine. Grandpa emptied one of the water bottles we had packed and then passed it to me so I could pee in it. "Just like camping," he whispered. "But no marshmallows." I knew he was trying to lighten the mood because we had no idea what we were going to do.

Grandpa decided that we should wait them out. He had faith that Jones would figure something out. We weren't sure how much time passed, but the two of us were so exhausted from stress that we eventually dozed off in the amusement ride cars.

We hadn't been asleep long when we heard a gentle tap on the truck. "Get ready," a voice said. "As soon as the door opens up, run into the show, not away from it."

"Hey, rube!" the voice then shouted. We immediately recognized those words as the carny call for help.

Suddenly, there was a tremendous ruckus. Men and women were shouting, and we could hear people scuffling about outside the truck once again. After a rush of footsteps, there was an ear-ringing sound of glass breaking.

When the truck door was yanked open, I was shocked to be staring at Bear. "Go!" he said under his breath.

We didn't hesitate to do exactly as told. Without looking back, Gramps and I ran straight back onto the lot and ducked behind a stack of boxes to catch our breath. From our vantage point, we witnessed the ensuing chaos.

There were several police vehicles stopped near the truck where we had been hiding. Their rooftop light bars shed gaudy hues of color over the entire area, while a group of officers stood watch nearby, scanning the area with flashlights.

"Look what our carny friends are up to!" Gramps said in awe. "Almost everyone we have met here has shown up to help us."

"I'm confused. What exactly are they doing?"

"They're throwing bottles at the fence on this side only, but not beyond. That way, they cannot be accused of attacking the police. Those clever devils are trashing their own property to create confusion and distraction."

As the upheaval continued, suddenly something caught the attention of the cops, who turned in unison to look. Under the lights, two silhouetted figures were visible. After a moment of hesitation, the figures stepped out of the shadows and ran down the hill toward the creek with the cops in pursuit.

"They're our acrobats," a voice whispered from behind. I jerked my head around to see Melba crouching behind us.

"My lord, Melba, you nearly caused me to have a seizure!" Grandpa gasped.

"I'm so sorry to startle you! As soon as you ran into trouble, Jones came around and alerted us all."

"Why are those acrobats running through the woods?"

"To distract the cops so they'll think they're you and Rainy."

"Look! The police are following them down the path that goes to the creek!"

"They'll never catch them. Those gymnasts will disappear into the woods where they can scale up trees so fast they'll never be seen. Hopefully, the authorities will think you made it out of the area, so they will have no reason to come back around. Our two decoys will join up with us again as soon as the coast is clear."

"I can't tell you how relieved I am," Gramps said. "But now everyone is involved in our troubles. They're bound to arrest Jones for harboring us--or those two people they think are us--in the first place."

"They can't," Melba smiled triumphantly. "Didn't you notice that our phony fugitives first appeared at the edge of the woods? No one can ever claim they were here on carnival grounds."

"That's true!"

"Jones came up with the idea."

"He took a tremendous risk for us."

"No need to worry about Jones. He's a crafty cuss. Look at him out there prowling like a tiger along the fence line. He knows not to cross any boundaries or push too far, but I promise you, he's enjoying every minute of this."

"What happens to Gramps and me now?"

"If everything goes well, they'll be searching for you somewhere else. You'll need to hide out here until we jump to our next location. Then it will be best if you stay with the show and live with us in safety until Primrose can get the situation resolved."

"You mean we would travel with the show?"

"Yes, honey. I'm sure Gramps would agree." Melba looked to my Grandfather for a response. "You know it's best, Reese. No one can live life on the run, especially a teenage girl."

"I'm afraid she's right, sweetheart. We can't go on like this."

"Gramps, I've enjoyed staying here, but joining the carnival is not something we ever talked about. It was fun because it was temporary. It's a life that's outside the norm. I'm not ready to be so ... so different."

My grandfather did not respond. I saw in his eyes that he was waiting for me to grasp the truth of what I had become. I *was* different. My old persona had disappeared into the night as quickly as my decoy had. My circumstances made me as different from the average person as many of the folks who had become our carny friends. The slow realization was confounding.

Gramps squeezed my hand, and then he nodded to Melba.

"Com'on," Melba urged as she pulled us toward the bright lights. "You're with us now."

I stumbled after her, uncertain yet acquiescent. We were joining the carnival, a decision that was strange and unexpected. I would be one of *them*--the freaks, the oddities, the performers, the rousties, the lost, the found, the grifters, and the saints—the *others*. Carnies.

BOOK II: BAKING SODA AND VINEGAR

21

ON THE ROAD - 1952

Two years went by quickly, and so did my sixteenth birthday. I was no longer the child who once strolled the carnival grounds with Tommy, wide-eyed and naïve. All our travels had provided me with advanced maturity and a more extensive education than I ever received in public school. I enjoyed the uncommon situation of living with my best friends, an opportunity most teenagers never experience.

Representing a mixture of races and ages, my friends were of all ages and from all parts of the country, each offering their own quirky perspective on life. Within the confines of our nomadic existence, carnies could be themselves, no matter how eccentric or physically unique that might be.

It would be dishonest, however, if I were to pretend to be fond of all my fellow travelers. Several rousties were standoffish, cranky, or downright troublemakers. And as anyone might suspect, there were a few who thought they were better than those whose bodies had been altered by accident or by Mother Nature.

Although disparaging remarks were sometimes mumbled in passing, the insults remained at a minimum. Everyone knew Jones would not tolerate disrespect.

Melba confided which employees were cheating the customers by shortchanging them, which she called "cake-cutting." She said a few others knew who the culprits were, but there was a code of silence unless their dishonesty became extreme enough to reflect upon the show.

Some of the ride jocks made money by cutting the rides short so they could run more rides, and workers who ran games often paid shills to move amongst the crowds looking for easy marks. I kept my distance from the arrogant and dishonest ones to avoid trouble.

Naturally, there were other downsides to our peripatetic existence as well. When we were on the road, I often felt the curious stares of locals who knew we were with the carnival. The harsh reactions of outsiders were even more exaggerated for the most physically distinctive carnies, so they seldom dared venture beyond the carnival grounds for fear of being humiliated, taunted, and even banned from some locations for being unsightly.

On rare occasions, Gramps and I ventured into new towns along the carnival booking route, but only when we were somewhere beyond the borders of New York State. As often as possible, we visited local museums and parks, and then Gramps relaxed somewhere nearby while I roamed through drugstores looking at teen magazines, paperback books, and cosmetics. (Beautiful Esther, the exotic sword swallower, had taught me how to apply just the right amount of mascara and rouge.)

Bugg had restored an old record player for me, so I occasionally picked up a new 45 record. When I saw other teenagers browsing through the record shelves, I felt like a foreigner. Often I would pretend to be browsing when I was secretly observing how they behaved and related to each other. Although their style of life seemed strange to me, it often made me long for the piece of myself I left behind the night we fled from our home. It was a life I knew I could never have again.

I was aware that Gramps agonized about our predicament, which was a situation neither one of us would have chosen. When he asked me how I truly felt about missing out on proms, football games, sleepovers, high school pep rallies, and all the other things that kids my age like to do, I confessed there were fleeting moments when I struggled with a sense of loss.

"But Gramps, we both know we took the 'road less traveled' because we were forced to choose this path to survive. You taught me that it is impossible to take one road and still experience what the other path offers, which I know is true. So please don't worry about me, because the road we're on is one constant adventure."

"Like a carnival ride?" he asked with a smile.

"Precisely! It's like an endless ride on Big Eli!"

———

Gramps and I felt safe when we set up in other states along the eastern seaboard because we weren't as recognizable as we once were, and to our knowledge, no one was looking for us outside of Broome County, New York. However, when the carnival had its yearly stint in Endicott, we were extra careful not to be seen.

During those two June weeks, Gramps and I seldom ventured from our wagons as a necessary precaution to avoid being spotted by any locals who might recognize us. Gramps did his bookkeeping work, and I designed new flyers for the show.

The limited verbal communication skills of Bugg and Earl had made me an expert at reading the silent language of others. I knew Primrose was in love with Gramps, and I was sure he felt the same way about her. And Prim was more like a mother to me than anyone in my life since my own mother died.

One night after we first joined the carnival, I came up with what I thought was an ingenious idea. I suggested to Gramps that he and Prim get married, and then they could foster me, as I was still considered a minor ... although that term felt like a misnomer when applied to me, as I had left childhood behind long before.

Although Gramps loved the idea of finding a solution, he reminded me he was a wanted man, so the first thing to be resolved was the charges against him. "Besides, I think it would be a lot for Primrose to take on, honey," he added. "She would be scorned for being with a white man because most of society denigrates mixed couples, and she can't jeopardize her job. She needs that money for Earl's care." I understood his position, but I made a mental note that he did not deny he would marry her under different circumstances.

Besides Primrose, Melba also was motherly to me. Prim and Grandpa watched over me, but it was Melba who taught me how to live life on the road.

Melba was only thirty-six years old, but I worried about her health and longevity. Her bones easily snapped, and her weight had dropped to seventy-five pounds. Recently, she broke her wrist simply by lifting a heavy book. But Melba always laughed it off when something like that happened.

"Ironically, I was reading a book about rocks," she joked.

"From now on, I'm restricting my reading to the subject of cotton." After the accident, Jones limited her work to operating the kiddie train ride from inside the ride's dog house.

While Melba was healing, a newbie was assigned her chore of helping me clean ride cars. The new ride jock, who I guessed to be about thirty years old, was named Zachary, but he went by just "Zee." He had only been with the carnival for two weeks, but I already sensed he was trouble.

I hated the way Zee looked at me or made suggestive sounds whenever I passed him by. Although I was pleased that my figure had developed significantly during the two years since our arrival, I did not want him undressing me with his eyes.

On his first day of ride maintenance, I explained the routine Melba and I had perfected. "If you want to do the seats, I'll get the rear."

"I'll be happy to get your rear," he snickered while shooting me an oily grin.

Not only was he lascivious, but he was also dishonest. He cleaned haphazardly and pocketed the money he found. I avoided complaining about anything to Jones, so I told Zee I could clean the cars by myself if he wanted to do something else. I hoped he would go away somewhere to slack off, and fortunately, he did.

Those of us with healthy bodies aided the others as much as we could. Besides Melba, many of our other friends who billed themselves as freaks or human oddities had health challenges.

My close friend Croak, a dwarf my age who had joined the show one week after Gramps and I did, was having serious stomach and colon ailments because his organs were confined to such a constricted space. However, he refused to go to a doctor. Like the other carnies, Croak was apprehensive about leaving the lot and was skeptical of outside doctors.

"There's them, and there's us," he said. "And they're not us."

That was a fact that was becoming clearer every day. It was a truth that would soon upend my life.

22

CURTAINS DOWN

Because Primrose could only join us on location periodically, I became her brother Earl's primary assistant for his hygiene routine. Sometimes Bugg helped me because it required more than one person, and Gramps was busy working in the office. Earl's growths were rapidly overtaking more areas of his body, and without proper cleansing, there was much more danger of infection. He had lost a tremendous amount of weight, which concerned everyone.

In my off hours, I loved spending time in Earl's wagon, watching with fascination as he used his claw tool and tweezers to assemble his model airplanes. On other occasions, I would recite to him from the books he lent me, which included John Steinbeck, William Faulkner, and Charles Dickens.

During my two years traveling with the carnival, Earl and I had become close with very few words. His appearance no longer scared me because, as Gramps said, I was learning to see with fresh eyes.

Earl was still performing, but it was apparent that singing had become increasingly more difficult for him. His performances were quite infrequent, so Gramps took over as the main musical act, which always revved up the crowd.

During the last two weeks of July, the carnival was set up just outside Lambertville, New Jersey, near the Delaware River. It was a beautiful, historic area that Gramps and I were planning to explore after the Sunday gathering. Earl was going to perform that day for the first time in weeks, so Gramps had already gone to the bally stage to help set up.

Primrose, who was making the drive from Endicott, wouldn't be arriving in time to assist, so I went over to Earl's trailer early to help him bathe. I also wanted to return a book by William Makepeace Thackeray called "Vanity Fair." I enjoyed the book so much that I placed paper markers between the pages with my favorite passages so I could read them to Earl.

When I recited, I used different voices, and on some occasions, I even threw in a bit of amateur acting for fun. Often Bugg joined us, and we had great times conversing with few words and lots of animation.

When I arrived, Earl was still in bed, which surprised me. Usually, he was in his pajamas waiting in his chair.

"Good morning," I said cheerfully. "Let me help you up, Earl. I hope you don't mind that I'm a little early."

I turned on the radio as I poured warm water into the basin and gathered washcloths and soap. "Oh, listen, Earl, that's Bing Crosby singing, 'At Last.' You love Bing Crosby!"

When I glanced over at him, he was still lingering in bed. "Come on now," I urged, "Prim is on her way and everybody's looking forward to your performance today. It has been too long since we heard you sing. Let's sit you up. I brought you some juice, so why don't you take a sip while I gather your clothes."

Bugg entered the trailer just as I got Earl into an upright position. Bugg was carrying a new easel and a handful of paint-brushes because the three of us often did watercolors together.

"Sing," Bugg managed to blurt in his usual one-word greet-ing, acknowledging Earl's upcoming performance. I was never bothered by the inability of my friends to speak more than a few words, or in Earl's case, none at all. There were occasional utterances, but I was happy with the silence.

"Thanks for bringing the art supplies. Our lazy friend is moving slowly today," I told Bugg. "Can you get his pajama shirt off for me?"

After Bugg set the easel down, he sat next to Earl on his bed and patted him on the shoulder. I always marveled at how a man as large as Bugg could be so gentle.

I had just put the kettle on for tea when I noticed Bugg struggling to get Earl undressed. Earl was limp and appeared to be panting. As Bugg pulled him forward to slip his shirt off, Earl suddenly gagged.

When I heard the loud choking sounds, I froze in place. "Earl, what's wrong? Bugg, why is Earl making those noises?"

Earl's attempts to breathe became more desperate as the choking continued. "Keep him upright, Bugg! Lift his arms over his head!"

By the time I ran to the bed, Earl's eyes were glazing over. "What's wrong, Earl? Breathe!" I screamed.

It was obvious Bugg was just as shocked and scared as I was. "Bugg did he eat anything? Is he choking on something?"

Bugg shook his head adamantly, and then he slapped Earl between his shoulders. When the choking became so acute that Earl began flailing his arms, Bugg picked him up from behind and squeezed his diaphragm. None of our attempts to relieve Earl worked. Bugg and I both fell into a state of panic. It was obvious we were losing him.

Bugg set Earl back down on the bed and ran out of the trailer to get help. In a last-minute effort to save Earl, I reached for his mouth to clear his throat. It was hard to find his lips because the growths had overtaken his face. "Help me, Earl," I pleaded, "help me!"

When I finally found the opening to his throat, I barely managed to get my index finger inside. I tried to clear his mouth, but there was no opening. I was shocked at what I felt. His esophagus was so completely blocked that there was no airway passage. Earl's entire throat was a mass of tumors.

I looked into his eyes, and at that moment, I knew he was telling me goodbye. He gently pushed my hand away from his face, and then he pressed it against his disfigured chest for a moment as his eyes slowly clouded over.

Earl squeezed my hand once more, and then the gagging ended, along with his lifelong struggle to exist in a world that considered him a freak.

———

By the time Bugg rushed back in, I had covered Earl with a sheet and was sitting motionless in a chair with my book in my lap. Bugg had Jones and Gramps in tow, and I could hear a siren in the distance.

When Primrose finally arrived, her cries were so painful that I fled from Earl's trailer to block out the sound. It's hard for me to remember too much of what happened after that. Somehow I disappeared into my head and couldn't focus on anything or anyone.

When Gramps caught up with me, I was sitting on the

bally stage staring out at the amusements. It seemed ironic that I was still holding Earl's copy of "Vanity Fair," a novel about trivial people with shallow values who could never have loved or appreciated a man like Earl. He was an aberration of nature in a world where beauty is valued over virtue. But to those who loved him, and I was one, Earl was beautiful.

23

AN UNEXPECTED HITCH OR TWO

Many times in my life I heard the adage "Sometimes good comes from bad." I never believed that to be anything other than a way to rationalize negative circumstances until Earl died.

We had a quiet service for Earl on the carnival grounds early one morning before the show opened. Sim and Bear sang a beautiful rendition of "Nearer My God To Thee" while Gramps accompanied them on piano. Jones said the eulogy, after which many of us added a word or two about how kind and brave Earl was. Primrose was too heartbroken to speak.

The statement made by my friend Croak touched me the most. "I may be a dwarf, but Earl made me feel tall. His words became a song, and his song was pure." I held onto that thought because it gave me so much comfort.

After the service, Primrose accompanied Gramps and me back to my wagon so we could speak in private. She was in a lot of pain, but she somehow managed to stay strong. When she said she planned to clear out Earl's wagon, I asked if I could keep his Steinbeck and Dickens books, as those were the novels he most often wanted me to recite. Although Earl couldn't express his feelings in words, I knew the quirky, eccentric characters in his favorite books lived in a world where Earl believed he would have been accepted.

Before Primrose left to tend to Earl's belongings, she updated us on her progress regarding our situation. For two years she had been fighting to clear Grandpa's name. The city councilman for whom she worked was very encouraged about being able to persuade authorities to drop the charges against Grandpa if he would turn himself in. I would then need to file a document stating that I left Endicott of my volition.

At first, we were excited to hear the news until we learned there was a hitch. I would have to go into the foster system while they cleared my grandfather's name. That created further complications because once the charges against Gramps were dropped, he would still be considered too old to foster me, especially with no mother figure at home. Primrose qualified as a foster mother, but she was informed that she could never take me in because of her color. Therefore, we were back where we started.

At that point in our lives, after two years on the run, I wasn't even sure I wanted to leave anymore, but I was tired of feeling like a hunted animal. Although the carnival had become my home, I didn't want to spend the rest of my life watching out for predators. And I didn't want to lose Primrose.

"Prim, now that Earl has passed, does this mean we won't be seeing you much anymore except during the two weeks each year when we're in Endicott?"

When I noticed Gramps look down at his hands, I realized I had voiced his same thoughts and concerns. We both knew our lives would not be the same without Primrose.

"Now, don't you go worrying about that," she reassured me. "Losing Earl left a huge hole in me. His absence made me stop to figure out what I want for my future. I loved him beyond words, and his care was my main purpose in life, but now I have to find a new direction. I'm going to quit my job."

"I thought you liked your job."

"Oh honey, that office is full of pasty-looking stuffed shirts. I have a nice nest egg, and because I no longer have to provide for Earl, I'm not as dependent on my salary as I once was. But don't you worry, because I plan to stay in contact with Councilman Anthony until we can finally resolve your situation."

"Prim, where will you get the money to live?" Gramps asked.

"I am the beneficiary of Earl's life insurance policy, Reese. I won't be rich, but I will have enough. And I can save money by giving up my apartment."

"Your apartment? Where are you going?"

"With you all."

My confusion was just as great as Grandpa's. "You're joining the carnival? Don't you have to be a performer or a roustie or something?"

"Yes, usually, but I plan to be someone's wife."

I was even more bewildered. "Whose wife?"

"Your grandfather's wife, if that silly man would stop staring at his hands long enough to ask me to marry him."

I turned to Grandpa, who looked shocked and thrilled all at the same time. "Say something, Gramps!"

"You know that is what I want, Primrose, but I don't want to complicate your life."

"Reese, I no longer need to protect my brother or my job. And we don't have to worry about discrimination from others because we can live here in what you refer to as a 'democratic commune.' I just need to put a fire under you, you old goat.

And of course, I also want Rainy's permission for us to get hitched."

"But this old goat is considered a criminal, Prim."

"Not by those of us who know you and love you. You may be a wanted man, but I want you more than the others."

Her announcement came out with such a surprising clatter that even a logical person would have thought Santa and his reindeer had landed on the roof. Her face was lit up the entire wagon.

"So are you two gonna get up off your seats and come over here and give ol' Primrose a hug, or are you just gonna leave me sitting here like yesterday's leftovers?"

"Yes, we'll marry you!" I yelled as I threw myself at her.

Gramps slowly rose from his chair, walked over to where she was sitting, and offered her his hand. When she stood up, I stepped aside so they could embrace. I watched in silence, unsure of what my grandfather's next response might be.

Grandpa held Prim for a long moment before a huge smile spread across his face. He then began to hum a familiar tune in her ear, and soon they were dancing and singing aloud, "Life is just a bowl of cherries ..." As I walked out of the wagon, I was humming as loudly as they were.

24

CELEBRATIONS

It was thrilling to discover that carny weddings are like a carnival within a carnival. Grandpa and Prim waited three months to marry out of respect for Earl, and by then, almost everyone was excited about the celebration.

As always, we had to hold the ceremony in the morning before the carnival opened for business. We had just arrived at a location near Daytona, Florida, a new stop Jones had set up along our travel route.

I had never been to Florida, and as excited as I was to see the ocean, I was worried about deadly snakes, alligators, crocodiles, and flying bugs rumored to be the size of a breadbox. "They're so big they have private airport landing strips," Jones grunted.

Prim informed us that Jones, whose first name was a mystery, was fond of Florida because it was his birthplace. He got summer work with a carnival when he was a teenager, but then he decided to stay on, so he dropped out of school to seek adventure on the road.

Within ten years, Jones proved himself to be so excellent at management that the carnival showman for whom he worked groomed him to take over his position. When Jones's employer was drafted into World War II, Jones, who was designated 4-F and thus unable to serve due to his physical anomalies, continued as manager of the show. Unfortunately, his boss was one of thousands of American servicemen who did not return from the front, which is how Jones became a showman.

It was a shock to Jones to learn the business had been left to him, but he worked hard to live up to his employer's expectations. Although he didn't tolerate any shenanigans, almost everyone liked him and respected him.

Jones could sometimes be ornery, but deep down inside, he had the same celebratory spirit as the rest of us, so he was equally excited about Grandpa's wedding. He asked Reno to bake a wedding cake, and then he sent two rousties out for champagne.

Daytona was especially hot for September, but that did not deter the carnies from showing up for the ceremony at the bally stage. Almost everyone was decked out in colorful outfits that included feathers, hats, and even a few tiaras. Even the dogs that traveled with the show were dressed for the occasion, as Melba, a fan of "canine couture," had fashioned bow ties and lace collars for them.

Croak, as spirited as ever, was wearing an old silk top hat, which was comical in proportion to his height. His head wobbled so much that in a strong breeze, he would have needed neck splints.

Melba wove flower garlands for Primrose and me to wear in our hair, and Grandpa insisted on wearing one as well because he didn't want to be "underdressed." Melba created his out of large sunflowers, which evoked a lot of cheers when he showed up for the celebration.

Gramps predicted a carnival wedding to be better than

Mardi Gras, and as always, he was right. When it was time for the ceremony, it was Bear, donned in a sequined vest, who read the vows.

I was surprised to learn that Bear had been ordained as a minister by some obscure but state-approved church that exchanges licenses for cash donations. He told us he did it on a whim when he discovered their advertisement in the back of a magazine. Bear was always full of surprises.

Bear, in his usual emcee fashion, added hilarious touches to the ceremony. After he introduced himself as The Righteous Reverend Bear, he made Gramps swear on the "Kama Sutra" that he would always be faithful to Prim. Then, after administering the vows, he pronounced, "And now *I* may kiss the bride."

Everyone hooted as Bear grabbed Gramps and planted a loud smack on his cheek. When Gramps pretended to swoon, Prim gestured to Bear that she was next in line. While the crowd hooted, Prim and Gramps finally sealed their vows with a kiss.

At the end of the ceremony, Melba, who was the Pied Piper of Dogs, jumped up on the stage and whistled. There was a stampede of paws as the canine brigade scrambled across the wood stage and gathered around Bear and the newlyweds. Clusters of dollar bills protruded from the dogs' collars and bow ties as they pranced around looking for hand-outs. (The sartorial cash accents were wedding gifts from the carnies.) One miniature bulldog, new to the circuit, decided to abscond with his loot, but the others stayed for the reception.

Jones popped a few corks and we all toasted the bride and groom. I loved the way Gramps smiled at Prim. Her dark skin and zaftig figure were a contrast to his pale complexion and thin frame, and yet they were a perfect match. Grandpa seemed fully relaxed for the first time since we arrived. I only wished my dad could have been there to see the happiness on his father's face.

Their joy simply added to my private euphoria. I was harboring a secret that I was not ready to share with anyone, because I didn't have the words to articulate what I felt.

25

AN UNCONVENTIONAL EDUCATION

Among those who lived in the carnival, there were only a few under the age of eighteen. Jones had a long-standing rule that anyone up to age sixteen was required to get a proper education. Before joining the carnival, "school fun" was an oxymoron to Croak and me. However, although we were over sixteen, we went to school anyway because carnival classes were so interesting.

Our classes were held between breakfast and chore time. Croak, who had purchased a bugle, played "Reveille" outside my wagon every morning to make sure I didn't oversleep, and because I laughed every time I heard him.

Croak always showed up at class wearing his top hat because he agreed with me that school was something to celebrate, and Croak was the type to celebrate everything. Due to his small stature, his diaphragm was compressed, so his voice sounded like squawking, which is how he got his nickname. He was hilarious, and I loved him dearly.

Croak's formal schooling ended when his father kicked him out of the house because his dwarfism was not only an embarrassment but also the cause of major medical expenses. When Croak wanted to join the carnival, Jones didn't ask many questions because he knew that people like Croak didn't have many resources for employment or education.

Fortunately, for both Croak and me, Jones was determined to provide educational opportunities. School was held in a trailer at the back of the lot. The previous summer, Croak and I had painted and rearranged the interior, so the makeshift classroom was pleasant and inviting.

During our decorating sessions, I learned about Croak's past. He confided that he once hated school because his elementary teachers often humiliated him by making him sing "I'm a Little Teapot" in front of the class.

"They insisted that my performances 'tickled the children.' My classmates laughed all right, but that's because I'm *shaped* like a teapot. I eventually found a way to convince the Nazi Wehrmacht of Education to drop the psychological torture tactics."

"You were only a kid. How did you persuade them?"

"Every time I sang 'when I get all steamed up' and the teapot whistled, I spit all over the floor."

"You didn't!"

"I sure did. I told them it's an affliction we dwarfs have when we sing. I even named it 'dwarf throat.' They were too over-concerned about sanitation and under-informed about teapot-shaped Lilliputians to know better," he laughed.

I loved how Croak addressed adversity with humor. It was a great lesson for me.

We had three other schoolmates who had been with the show for more than a year. Cassie, who was the same age as Croak and me, was Voluptuous Vivian's daughter. She moved in with the carnival after Vivian's ex-husband passed away. Cassie's father had taken custody of her and divorced Viv when he could no longer deal with Vivian's weight and appearance. As a result, Vivian and Cassie were practically strangers. Although I liked Cassie, I sensed she wouldn't be around for long. She had a runaway look about her, like a rabbit in a field full of coyotes.

Our other two classmates, shy twin boys named Jacob and Jeffrey, were eleven years old. They were the sons of Winston the Gentle Giant, who never even knew he had sons until they showed up at the gates looking for a home. Their mother, who had a severe drinking problem, had abandoned them, so Winston was happy to take them in even though they were strangers.

Although our classes were fun, they were certainly unconventional. Our teachers were other carnies, each expected to volunteer time if they had a talent to share or knowledge in a specific area of study. Our classes were never boring because each of the carnies brought what Croak dubbed a "living education."

Gramps knew a tremendous amount about both World Wars, so together with Esther, who had lived in France, they taught us European history. Esther also gave lessons in Spanish and French. And Gramps taught us everything he knew about math, bookkeeping, and landscaping-including bugs, birds, flowers, trees, and weather patterns.

My grandfather was full of obscure facts that made learning exciting. He explained that for a few months during WWII, sliced bread was banned in an attempt to conserve steel used in slicing machines, a law that was rescinded after three months of public outcry. Then in what he referred to as an "ancillary exercise," he taught us how to make bread in Reno's oven, despite Reno's grumbling.

As a challenge to us to research for answers, Gramps set up bets on questions that we had to prove with theorems. Croak

BEYOND THE HOLE IN THE FENCE

lost a bet with Gramps when he learned that hail is usually formed during summer. As payment for the bet, Croak was supposed to teach us something weather-oriented. He surprised Gramps by performing a hilarious rendition of Lena Horne's "Stormy Weather" while wearing a dress and acting out the lyrics. It was not educational, but it sure was funny.

Jones was an authority on the War of 1812 and the Civil War because he had read so many books on those subjects. He told us that the term Uncle Sam was named after New York meat merchant Samuel Wilson who sent boxes of meat to the troops in the War of 1812. They were all stamped with the letters U.S., which became Uncle Sam. We loved all the color he added to each lesson.

We were riveted each time Jones got all wound up while describing gripping battles like Bull Run and Gettysburg. My favorite moment was when he "died" on the trailer floor after a direct hit by a Remington 1858 cap and ball revolver. It was a prolonged and agonizing death.

Prim did her part by teaching typing, shorthand, and some of my favorite classes, which were about the history of Negroes in the South. She did "plantation tours" using a map, and at every imaginary stop, she taught us the history of the area and even prepared a few Southern dishes for us to sample. (By the time we "arrived" in New Orleans and demanded gumbo, Reno gave up the fight for his kitchen and promised to teach a cooking class next year.)

We had music and physical education as well. Sim, who when he wasn't "flying" rolled around on a board with wheels, gave us vocal lessons. Bugg silently taught us to paint and whittle, and Sorrel, the acrobat who had acted as my decoy during our escape attempt, taught us gymnastics on the lawn.

Winston, the father of the twins, was steeped in knowledge about Native American Indians. For the first time, history came alive for me and was not just a bunch of useless statistics to be memorized for tests. (Tests were never a factor in carnival school, as the State did not interfere with our education, which was another advantage of being nomadic.)

Each carny who taught was committed to teaching us about the world outside our insular existence. They all contributed to a wide-ranging education, but none more than Bear.

26

BERRILL PATRICK DEANE

Bear, our best bally stage talker, had a knack for direction and organization, so Jones asked him to be the de facto Program Director for the school. He taught classes also, and I was surprised to learn he was a serious writer who had penned several travel articles he was trying to get published. He liked drama and reading, so Croak and I had lively discussions with Bear about our favorite novels and plays.

Not quite twenty, Berrill "Bear" Deane was 3 1/2 years older than I, and very well traveled. On school days, Bear and I always arrived earlier than the others because we both relished the break from the hustle and bustle of carnival existence.

Bear set up a record player in the school trailer so we could listen to records while setting up. I loved to hum along with him to "Tell Me Why" by the Four Aces, which was one of Bear's favorite songs. Sometimes he even belted out the lyrics, which was always a cheerful way to start the day. When he was in an especially upbeat mood, he entertained me with his spot-on impersonations of Marlon Brando as Stanley Kowalski in "Streetcar Named Desire," which always delighted me.

During our quiet time, I learned a lot about his background. Like me, Bear had lost his parents at an early age, so he could not escape the foster system. The people he lived with did not take in foster children out of kindness, but because they needed farm hands. According to Bear, the labor was intense, food was scarce, and the beatings were frequent.

When he finally decided to escape, Bear stole his guardian's wallet and an extra pair of shoes, and then he jumped out a second-story window into the back of an abandoned flatbed truck parked below. As soon as he reached the highway on foot, he hitched rides to get as far away from Texas as he could.

He was only fourteen years old when he hitchhiked from the watermelon fields of Texas to the cranberry fields of New Jersey. He lived in an apartment with several other runaways, which he described as "a foster home with no fostering." The disparate group of roommates shoplifted for necessities, played basketball on the public courts, and on a whim, took free acting classes at the local community theater.

After several years, however, Bear grew tired of field labor and decided he wanted to see more of the world. One night of amusement at a local carnival was all he needed to find his direction. With his bit of stage experience and his gift of gab, he thought he could land a better-paying job as a carnival talker. Jones hired him six months before Gramps and I arrived.

To me, Jones was a brilliant proprietor because he had seen Bear's potential. Or maybe I was just grateful because, from the day I first saw Bear, I felt emotions I had never experienced before. Like my true identity, I kept my feelings secret. I didn't want anyone to know I was in love with Bear Deane.

27

THE STORM

Many folks who were in South Carolina during August 1952, were overtaken by such terrifying forces of nature that their night dreams still occur, bringing waves of terror along with mental images of the destruction. I am one of those people.

Although we had pulled into town three days earlier, all the trailers that carried the amusement rides were still battened down, as Jones had deemed it wise not to erect anything until we received better weather reports. Not only could heavy winds damage the rides, but the constant rain would discourage visitors, so despite the daily revenue losses, there was no value in risking the expensive equipment.

Due to another day of inclement weather warnings, school was not in session either. Storm clouds hovered above, cloaking the morning sky with a blanket of darkness and resulting in continuous alerts about an offshore tropical storm.

As I exited my wagon, I saw Gramps and Prim, who were on their way to the office. "The storm is rolling in, Rainy," Gramps cautioned. "Get your breakfast quickly and get on back to your wagon before those clouds dump all over us again. I've never seen so much water!"

"I'm hurrying, Gramps."

"If the winds get too bad, you come on over and spend the day with me. The Big Bedford truck that houses the office is much more secure than the wagons.

"Will do! You and Prim stay dry today too. Love you!"

I was nearing the kitchen area when it began to rain again. As I struggled with my umbrella, a gust of wind hit me with such force that it turned my umbrella inside out. To avoid being drenched, I ran to the picnic tables where Croak and several other carnies were huddled under the tent, their gaze fixed on the looming clouds above. There were deep puddles all around the area from the night rains, and I could see Reno inside the kitchen mopping up water.

"Good morning, Rainy," Croak said.

"Good morning. No top hat today?"

"Too windy, but I'm just as handsome without it, right?"

"I'd have to agree with that. I almost mistook you for that movie star, Tab Hunter."

"Common mistake, I'm afraid. I'm constantly mistaken for one of those teen idols. I suffer in silence."

Croak always made me smile. I had become so accustomed to his misshapen, dwarf body that I barely noticed his awkward gait.

"I already ate so I'm heading back to my wagon. Come join me later and we can play cards while we wait out the storm."

"That sounds like fun. See you soon."

As I was pouring a cup of coffee, I heard someone chuckling behind me. "I don't think that thing will be very effective today, Rainy." When I turned around, Bear was pointing at my umbrella. "Your umbrella has already given up the fight."

"My umbrella is smarter than I am," I laughed.

"I guess there are a few of us who just can't go without our morning coffee or Reno's banana pancakes."

"I think you can forget those today, Bear. Reno has his hands full sopping up puddles. This weather is a mess. I'll bet the school trailer is leaking too."

"I'm sure you're right. It's nothing but an old tin can with a rusted-out roof."

"I hope everything doesn't get ruined. All our books and papers are sitting out on the tables."

"Hmm ... I forgot about that. We can't lose our collection of books or those new encyclopedias. I'll run on over there and shove everything into the metal file cabinets so nothing gets ruined."

"You'll need help. I'll meet you there in ten minutes. We'd better hurry!"

———

Bear and I were placing the last of the books into a trunk when Zee yanked open the trailer door. As my eyes adjusted to his image in the doorway, thunder shook the trailer, and lightning flashed through the sky, framing Zee with an eerie and threatening light. He was strangely unfazed by the onslaught of rain. It was almost as if he enjoyed being pelted by the punishing sheet of water.

Bear shot me a curious look when he saw me move as far away from Zee as I could. Although Zee was attractive in a rough-and-tumble way, he was crude, and he made me very uncomfortable. I hated the way he bullied people. He often knocked Crock's top hat off his head, and several times he hid the rolling cart Sim used for mobility when he wasn't flying.

Earlier the preceding morning, after Croak awakened me with his bugle call, I opened the door of my wagon to a downpour. I told Croak to go ahead to class and get out of the rain while I grabbed some coffee and toast for both of us from the cookhouse.

After Croak waddled off, Zee appeared out of nowhere, as if he had been standing somewhere waiting and watching. I was completely unnerved when he followed me the entire way to the cookhouse. He stayed close behind me, making suggestive clicking sounds with his tongue until I had almost reached the tented area where the other carnies had gathered for breakfast. As I ducked out of the rain, I looked over my shoulder. Zee had vanished.

I was foolish to hope that would be an isolated incident, and yet I was shocked to see Zee suddenly reappear at the trailer door like a dark omen in the ominous storm.

"Hey, man," Zee said to Bear without looking my way, "I've got some free time to teach auto maintenance, which everyone should learn, even girls ... 'stuff like how to change your oil, fix a flat tire, and that sort of thing. So how 'bout if I give it a whirl?"

Bear glanced at me again before answering. "Thanks for offering, man. I'll give it some thought for the schedule."

As soon as Zee left, Bear and I silently packed up the supplies. It wasn't until we were closing up the trailer that Bear said, "I'll walk you back to your wagon, Rainy. And stay away from Zee if you can. I don't trust that oily turd."

———

When Bear opened the door, the harsh wind blew torrents of rain in our direction. He shoved it closed before we could get soaked. "I think we better wait until the rain and wind die down. While we've been in here packing up, the storm kicked up with a vengeance."

"I'm not afraid to get wet. What if we run for it?"

"I've never seen winds like this. And I don't see anyone else out there, Rainy. I don't think we should risk it." Bear tried to peer out again, but he couldn't hold the door open against the angry gusts of wind that pushed him back inside.

"You better lock the door. Hopefully, we will be safe in here."

Although it was morning, the interior of the trailer was growing darker by the minute. When Bear tried the light switch, there was no electricity. I could hear the wind whistling outside, causing the trailer to rattle loudly. He and I looked at each other in silence as we contemplated our next move. The heavy rain that lashed at the trailer sounded like a locomotive barreling down the tracks.

Suddenly, the trailer started shaking. As I tried to hide my panic, I suppressed my urge to flee. I knew there was nowhere to go. "I'm scared, Bear," I whispered.

"Come over here next to me, Rainy. I won't let anything happen to you. We can't go out there now. Let's just wait it out."

Bear wrapped his arms around me and dragged me under a table just as the rain got so loud it sounded like gunfire. There was a loud, whistling sound, and then in a split second, the wind ripped the roof off the trailer.

Just as I screamed, the sky roared again. "The trailer is moving, Bear!"

Bear and I clung to the legs of the table as it slid across the floor. Then suddenly, the trailer tipped over on one side, and we tumbled together. We were still within the confines of its metal structure when another gust of rain and wind besieged us so fast that the trailer rolled, hurling us from one side to the other as though it couldn't decide where to discard our bodies.

Bear held me tightly as file cabinets, chairs, and tables

crashed all about us. When flying debris bit into his leg, Bear cried out in pain, but he kept a tight grip on me. As he pressed his chest against mine and clutched me to him, my body lurched with each blow to my back and legs.

I could feel the wind lift the trailer, and I knew we were about to roll once more. The instant the trailer became airborne, Bear and I were flung out onto the ground while the trailer crumpled like paper upon impact with a Mack truck.

Bear and I landed on a hard surface in what seemed to be a river of water. My head was near Bear's feet, so I reached out to grab his ankle.

Hurricane-powered winds split the sky into streams of flying debris. I was prepared to die when two powerful arms reached down to lift both Bear and me in one swoop.

Like two limp rag dolls, we were thrown into the back of one of the huge vans where we landed amongst a maze of iron gears. Somewhere in my mind, it registered to me that we were crouched in a gap between the side of a van and the support frame and cables of Big Eli. The Ferris wheel in its retracted state left little room for us to maneuver, but its vast weight also offered protection against the wind.

I was disoriented and unsure how I got there. But before I passed out, I heard Bear utter, "Bugg!"

28

AFTERMATH

When I came to, I slowly became aware that Bugg and Bear were squeezed into the van with me. My entire body was in tremendous pain from being pummeled during the storm. In the dim light, I saw that Bear had an open wound on his leg. Bugg had tied a rag around the blood-soaked area where the flying debris had ripped through Bear's jeans and into his skin.

Although we had been rescued, I was suddenly conscious of what had happened and was fraught with alarm. "Where's my grandfather?" I yelled as I oriented myself to my surroundings. I tried to stand up, but Bugg placed his hand firmly on my shoulder and shoved me back down.

"Safe. Stay."

There were oily canvases wrapped around the gears, which Bugg tucked in around me to stop my shivering. The three of us huddled together for more than twenty-four hours as the winds and rain continued with no mercy.

Bear and I were lapping up rainwater from the floor of the van when Bugg peered out the van door and then signaled that it was safe for us to make a run for it. Although the sirens continued to blare almost nonstop and it was still raining hard, the intensity of the storm had lessened enough for us to escape.

It was extremely difficult to stand. Bear was limping, and we were both bruised badly. On each of us, black pockets of blood had formed bulging welts that were threatening to push through the skin. From my reflection on the steel door of the van, I could see my face, a swollen and pulpy-looking mass, which was as distorted as Bear's.

As we crawled outside the van, we were shocked at the devastation. It was still raining and very windy as we made our way our way around the piles of metal and wood. I had never seen so much water and debris. Mother Nature had unleashed unspeakable wrath on the town of Beaufort.

The Mack vans were heavy enough not to have toppled over, but there were many overturned housing wagons and trailers on one side of the grounds where the winds had hit the hardest. There appeared to be less damage on the opposite side where my wagon was located. In the distance, I could see that my wagon and the other converted rail cars near it remained upright, clinging tightly to their heavy wheelbases.

The line of transport vans carrying the amusement rides had weathered the storm, although the winds had forced one of them into a nearly perpendicular position to the lineup. We bypassed several demolished concession stands while fighting our way to the safety of a group of Big Bedford trucks that were sheltered within a group of Mack vans.

As we approached the Bedford truck that housed the office, I spotted Gramps peering out the window of the entry door. When he saw me, he darted out and wrapped his arms around me tightly. "Rainy! Rainy!" he yelled.

I could no longer hold back my tears as I buried my face in

his neck. While the rain beat down upon us, he squeezed me so hard I moaned with pain.

"I'm sorry!" Gramps yelled into the wind. "I'm so sorry. Are you okay, Rainy? Are you hurt badly?" I could feel him shaking as he dragged me inside where I spotted Croak and Melba and many of our other friends who had huddled together for safety. I was also relieved to see that some of our pets were safe, although most were shaking with fear.

Melba and Primrose threw blankets around me, while Esther tried to console Dotty, the childlike pinhead, who began wailing as soon as she saw Bear and me. Jones ran forward to help Bugg move Bear inside, and then they immediately administered first aid on his leg.

"I don't think it's broken, Jones," Bear groaned.

"It doesn't feel like it, but it's a nasty wound and you're going to need a lot of stitches. Sterilize it and sew it up, Bugg," he directed.

"Do it, Bugg," Bear nodded.

"It's a wonder you two kids are alive!"

When Croak brought me a cup of water, I noticed that someone had applied a large bandage to his forehead. "Are you badly injured, Croak?" I asked. "That looks nasty. I hope you don't have a concussion."

"I'm just a little dazed, Barbara Sue, and my unicorn is missing, but no head damage to speak of," he grinned impishly.

"Very funny, you clown, but thanks for making me laugh." After I sipped the water, Croak then offered it to Bear.

Prim hugged me repeatedly while Melba gently checked my mud-caked limbs for wounds. My face, which felt grossly distended, throbbed so much that it was difficult to move my jaw.

It worried me to see how badly my grandfather's hands

were shaking. "Gramps, I'm okay now. I was very lucky. Bear protected me until Bugg found us. Thanks to them, I'm alive. I'm just battered."

"I just thank God you're not dead. I was so worried, Rainy! As the storm was growing out of control, Jones and I ran all over looking for you. Then, when the hurricane made landfall, the doors of the truck had to be locked for the safety of everyone else who had run here seeking shelter. I refused to come inside, but Bugg threw me into the truck and went back out to find you on his own."

"Bugg saved our lives," Bear said as watched the man responsible for our rescue gently scrubbing the long gash in his leg.

"He's a very brave man," Gramps nodded. "I'll never be able to repay you, Bugg."

Bugg, too humble to accept praise, continued tending to Bear without glancing up or acknowledging Grandpa's praise. We were all in awe of Bugg's bravery, and I'm sure Gramps and Bear felt the same way I did. I was filled with a tremendous love for that silent, selfless man.

———

The punishing hurricane that made landfall in Beaufort on August 31, 1952, did not dissipate until September 1.

Our location was on the opposite side of Mulligan Creek from Lady's Island, which sustained the greatest amount of damage from the storm. However, we suffered tremendously as well because of the inherent structural vulnerability of a traveling show.

After weeks of equipment repairs and labor-intensive replacements, our outfit eventually recovered enough to jump to a new location. Although those of us who were injured during the hurricane had recovered, as we prepared to move on, our roster was down by one.

During the twenty-four hours after the storm, Jones took a headcount and realized that several dogs were missing. Worst of all, so was Sim.

We pieced together enough information to learn that on the worst day of the storm, Croak had been the last person to see Sim on his way to the tent for his morning coffee. He said Sim was looking all over for his roller board, which was missing once again. Sim referred to the scooter as his "belly board" because he could lie on his stomach and push with his hands. It was his only other means of mobility when not using his arms to fly.

Croak offered to carry Sim on his back so he wouldn't have to swing from location to location during such high winds, but Sim, one of the most self-reliant people I had ever met, politely refused.

Sim always left his board by the steps that led up to his wagon, so he told Croak he was sure it must've blown underneath, insisting he could easily crawl under to get it. "I'm like a crab, Croak," he said. "It will only take me two seconds to get under there, so you go on ahead without me, and I'll catch up with you."

Sim never showed up at the cookhouse. As the storm was kicking up, Croak sought shelter in the Big Bedford, which was part of the emergency routine. As he fought his way through the wind and rain, he circled back past Sim's wagon, but Sim was nowhere to be found. Croak assumed he had already joined the others in one of the vans designated as shelters.

As soon as it was determined that Sim was missing, everyone joined in the search. It was heartbreaking when we finally spotted two rousties carrying Sim's body lifeless body, which they had located under a truck.

GWEN BANTA

Jones was sure that Sim was trying to get to one of the shelter trucks when he lost his life. Unable to find his belly board, which would have allowed him to travel close to the ground, Sim tried to flee by swinging from object to object. With only half a body, there was no way he would have been able to withstand the high winds.

We were all devastated by what happened to our dear friend. I was also tormented by a nagging thought I would never be able to prove, or dismiss. I was sure Zee had taken Sim's belly scooter as one of his bullying pranks, especially after the scooter turned up near the steps to Sim's wagon several days after Sim's body was located.

Alva, our bearded lady who was one of Sim's closest friends, believed the scooter had slipped under the wagon and was lodged loose during the extreme winds. I couldn't accept her theory, because it was too coincidental that the scooter would reappear in the exact place where Sim always kept it.

I knew in my heart that Zee hid the scooter as a sick prank, just as he had done many times before to taunt him. As a result of Zee's cruel bullying, Sim had no way to reach shelter other than to subject his undersized frame to the powerful and destructive hurricane winds. I could not bear the thought of how Sim must have died.

I hated Zee for what he had done, and when I ran into him again after the storm, instead of avoiding him, I fearlessly held my ground and stared him down. He knew I knew.

Zee grunted and walked away, but that was only the beginning of my problems with Zee.

29

ANOTHER BLOW

Recovery from the hurricane was difficult for all of us, but our crises were not over.

Not only had Jones lost a lot of money because of the damage from the storm and the downtime required for repairs, but there also was a series of other incidents that affected us all, inspiring Mariah, our fortuneteller, to claim we had been cursed. (Bear said her prophetic talents were dubious because any blockhead could make pronouncements about events that had already happened.)

It seems my talent for prophecy was better than Mariah's. I had predicted that Vivian's daughter Cassie would leave, and sure enough, she did. However, before sneaking away in the middle of the night, she stole all of Voluptuous Vivian's savings. Vivian was loved by everyone, so we were all very sad to hear what Cassie had done.

Due to her massive weight, Vivian often needed money to pay for the medical problems related to her hypothyroidism and resulting obesity, but Cassie left her with nothing. After Cassie's departure, Croak, Bear, and I referred to Cassie as "The

Artful Dodger" because, as Croak pointed out, she had a bright future as a gang leader.

Winston the Gentle Giant faced an even worse problem with his twins that ended up affecting all of us. Both boys started to complain of exhaustion, weakness, and terrible aches, especially in the neck area.

As soon as Winston mentioned it to Jones, Jones insisted that the boys be quarantined. Polio had been sweeping the nation, and even though it was more common for younger children to contract the crippling illness, it still occurred among kids who were the twins' age, as well as with adults.

It was unusual to bring in an outside doctor, but Jones did not want to take any chances. We had picked up three other minors during the past year so the school room was tight quarters, and therefore, a veritable Petri dish for polio.

Having just lived through the tropical storm disaster in South Carolina, we were now set up at a location in Augusta, Georgia. Jones knew a retired physician in the area whom he called first. When the doctor examined the boys, he diagnosed both with polio, which was tragic news to everyone. Winston and the twins immediately left the show so the boys could recover in a polio ward. As soon as they left, Jones immediately set up strict rules of quarantine to protect the rest of us.

Unfortunately, when the twins were isolated in a polio ward, the State Board of Health was alerted of cases of polio in our camp, so several State health authorities showed up at the grounds with an order that we all be tested to reduce the possibility of any further spread of the disease.

I planned to hide out while they were there, but Gramps insisted that I be examined like everyone else. "You cannot run away from this one, Rainy," he said. "I would rather take the risk of more trouble than the risk of you contracting polio, especially knowing you spent so much time with the twins in that school room day after day. I cannot bear the thought of you contracting a disease that can cause permanent paralysis and loss of lung function. You must go."

Polio terrified me too. I was horrified at the thought of lung paralysis that would require a prolonged period, or even a lifetime of complete confinement in a metal respirator tube just to be able to breathe.

A group of medical personnel set up a day to check us all. On the morning of their arrival, we formed a line, and then one by one, we were tested for fever and other symptoms that might flag us as carriers. The masked testers recorded the name and age of each of us before going through a checklist of questions regarding symptoms, background, and exposure. After the interview part, they took temperatures, tested reflexes, and examined throats.

As I waited my turn with Croak and Bear, Croak nudged me. "They're asking the minors a lot more questions than the adults because they were in school with the twins, and polio is affecting so many kids. Just to be safe, I think we better lie about our ages, Rainy. I don't want them probing into my background."

"I don't either!" I must have responded a little too sharply because Bear looked at me curiously. However, as someone familiar with a "no questions" lifestyle, he did not question my apprehension. Instead, when we got to the front of the line, he shoved me before him and said, "Please examine my wife Tony first."

I wasn't sure what Bear was up to, but I always knew I was safe if I just followed his lead. "My name is Tony Fuh-Ferris," I said, because the Ferris wheel was the only thing that came to mind at that moment. "My full name is Antoinette Ferris, age twenty-one."

The overworked examiner tilted her head somewhat curiously, but then Bear, being the expert talker that he was, engaged her in animated conversation to create a distraction. The woman then dismissed me without asking the more detailed questions reserved for minors.

Suddenly, it occurred to me that when Bear introduced me as his wife, he was implying I was of legal age, which was a clever move on his part. To my relief, the examiner found no reason for either of us to be suspected as carriers of the horrific disease.

As we exited the van where the examinations were taking place, Bear whispered, "Nice going, Miss Fuh-Fuh-Fuh-Ferris."

"Tony to you," I giggled. "You couldn't come up with a girl's name?"

"I had Frosted Flakes for breakfast, so all I could think of was Tony the Tiger."

"I suppose I should be relieved that you didn't have flap-jacks!" I grinned. I loved to tease Bear because I could make him blush, just as he so often made me do. But Bear had saved me from a sticky situation. And he had called me his wife. It was a very good day.

30

QUARANTINE

We weren't able to open the show the entire time we were in Delaware. We had been scheduled for a two-week run, but Jones was told he had to keep the show shut down for fourteen days after our last exposure to the twins.

Those of us who had been together at the school were allowed to spend the days together because we had already been exposed. Only Croak and I persisted in attending school, and Bear told the other teachers he would take over the teaching for those two weeks, as he had been the teacher most exposed to the twins.

A few canine students insisted on joining us as well. They were part of our motley group of stray "roadie dogs" who traveled the carnival circuit with us. They belonged to us all, although some of them attached themselves to specific carnies. Melba called them "carndogs," which I thought was very amusing.

Although I enjoyed all the dogs, there was one impish critter that I couldn't resist. My favorite little mutt, the same miniature bulldog mix that absconded with his collar stuffed with wedding cash, had recently become quite attached to Melba. He was equally hooked on the peanut butter cookies Melba carried around in her pocket.

The dog was so round and ugly that he was cute. He was an undersized dog with an oversized head and a pronounced underbite, which made the little guy look fierce despite his sweet demeanor. Because his lower teeth covered his upper teeth, when he barked, he sounded like a frog grunting the word "bat." Therefore, we dubbed him "Batts," which fit him perfectly because the dog was a little batty.

Batts loved to roll around in the dirt and chase his almost nonexistent tail. Melba, who tried to discourage the energetic dog from sleeping in her trailer, reported being awakened many nights by an intruder with a maniacal stare and a silly underbite that glowed in the dark. After repeated nighttime visits, Melba discovered that the squatty but determined little rascal somehow managed to climb on a barrel and crawl through her window.

She complained about the mutt, but I knew she adored him. We all did. Croak was very fond of Batts as well, so sometimes he walked around with the little critter hidden under his top hat. When he removed his hat, Batts squawked on command, and then Croak joined in, imitating Batt's bark perfectly.

As a reward, Melba usually gave each of them a piece of cookie. I promised Croak that if he could learn to chase his tail like Batts, I would give him an entire steak. The two devoted companions were always quite a show.

Batts followed Croak to our school trailer every day during quarantine, so Bear addressed him as one of the students, often asking him to "recite." Batts and his canine gang were a welcome diversion from the polio threat that loomed over us.

I can't say that much learning occurred during those two

weeks. We were not in the mood to study. After the trauma of the preceding month, our focus was relaxation and rejuvenation. Instead, we had long personal conversations that brought us closer together and underscored our sense of Family and Home.

Bear, Croak, and I shared as much as we were willing regarding our backgrounds and experiences, but I remained the most circumspect out of necessity. I had to protect Gramps, who was still a wanted man.

Prim was still working behind the scenes to get Grandpa's unofficial adoption of my dad "grandfathered in," but the days of waiting had stretched into two years of living under new identities in a most unusual existence.

However, I learned to love the freedom and camaraderie inherent to our carnival lifestyle. One day I asked Croak how he became connected with the show, assuring him that there was no need to reveal anything he wished to keep private. To my surprise, he was quite forthcoming.

"I'm not a whiner, but to be perfectly honest, being born into a body like this is something I would not have chosen. Every day of my life there is a new battle to fight. There are lots of health hurdles because my organs are compressed, but the biggest challenges have always been emotional."

"Were the health challenges just as bad when you were small?" I asked.

"No, but even when I was little, I knew I was different. People would say aloud, as if I had no ears, that I was a 'little funny face,' or 'an odd, but pleasant little fella.' Then I started hearing words like 'deformed.' As you know, people can be oblivious and ignorant."

"Did you attend a regular school?" Bear asked.

"Yeah, Bear, for as long as I could take it. But because my head is large and disproportionate to my body, I was called a 'retard,' or 'mushroom head,' or most often, 'Elmer Fudd,' like the cartoon character. At age twelve, when my voice lowered from a high pitch to the duck-like pitch I have now, that's when I was dubbed 'Croak' by a teacher."

"Would you like us to call you by a different name?"

"No, but thank you for caring. I became accustomed to the nickname and tried to use humor to my advantage by doing great imitations of Donald Duck. But just as I was learning to handle all the body shame by redirecting my embarrassment into humor, that's when the physical harassment started."

"Who mistreated you?"

"Well, remember, I'm small. I just look tall," he added with a smirk. "So by the time I entered junior high school, there were kids who were big enough to pick me up and throw me around as if I were a football. As with most of these situations, there was one ringleader. He was a moron named Ralph with a band of followers who quickly caught onto his sick game."

"What did your parents do about it?"

"They were both dwarves, and my father had already passed away after his intestine ruptured due to a colon blockage. My mother was very ill and weak, so we were both living at a church shelter. I never told her because she had enough to deal with, and I did not want to cause her any more pain."

"Couldn't the teachers help?"

"I don't think they wanted to know about the problem, let alone deal with it. People like me are seen as freaks by adults too, not just to kids. Adults may not be as overt in their responses and actions, but many either don't want to look at me, or they speak to me as though I'm mentally deficient. I even had a teacher ask if she could stroke my head because she heard that rubbing a little person on the head brings good luck."

That truly shocked me. "A teacher? Oh, my God! Did you let her?"

"I told her she was free to do it anytime but to beware of head lice."

Bear and I both laughed. From the first day I met Croak, I was captivated by his humor.

"But why join a carnival?" Bear asked.

"There was an incident that almost killed me, and after that, I just couldn't take it anymore. It happened as I crossed a bridge over the river that ran through our town, which was my daily route to school. One morning, Ralph and his group of thugs decided to follow me, hurling taunts as they got closer and closer.

"I wanted to run, but there was nowhere to go, and with my short legs, there was no way to outrun them. It only took them a few minutes to catch up with me, and by then, I was in a panic.

"Without warning, Ralph lifted me from behind, and they began their sick game of football, tossing me back and forth on the bridge. I was praying to God a car would come by because we were getting closer and closer to the edge. Finally, and intentionally, Ralph threw me over the bridge into the water below. 'Let's see if you can bob,' he laughed. To this day, I remember how sinister and angry he sounded, as if I had no right to live because I was an abomination he had to look at every day."

"I've never heard of such cruelty, Croak!"

"Yeah, it was terrifying, Rainy. I screamed for help because I had never learned how to swim. As I thrashed in the water, my compressed lungs could not provide enough oxygen, and after a prolonged struggle, I felt myself giving up. Then a sense of calm finally washed over me. I was suddenly floating far above the water as I watched myself go under, and I remember thinking, 'Oh, so this is how I'm going to die.'

"However, I was wrong. There was a man on the lower bank of the river who jumped in and pulled me to shore. He then pounded on my chest until I came to. When I looked up to the bridge, Ralph and his friends were gone. They didn't even care enough to see if I survived. The way I perceived the entire incident was that I must not be worthy of life."

"Man, Croak, I really admire you."

"Me?"

"Yes, you. Not many people would be strong enough to handle that kind of mental and physical abuse," Bear told him. "I'm not sure I would."

"Sure you would, Bear. You just don't know it. We handle what we have to until we choose to be done. And that day, I wanted to be done with life. I thought about jumping back into the river because I just wanted to be free."

"What changed your mind?"

"Ah, well, the guy who saved me was still standing there in his wet clothes, so throwing myself back into the water would have been a little disrespectful. Also--and take my advice on this--choose something other than drowning as your last exit. I recommend holding out for something like a hot fudge sundae overdose if you get a choice," he said with an impish grin. "Surely, it has to beat suffocation."

"That does sound like a better way to go," I nodded.

"Yep. And if a Good Humor ice cream truck had come by that day, I might be dead by now. Anyway, the worst was yet to come."

"There was something more awful than nearly drowning?"

"Yeah, Bear. To me, what happened next was even more painful."

———

I couldn't imagine what worse things Croak had to endure, and I also could not have measured his bravery. Like all the people in our carnival with physical anomalies, he had developed a strength and resilience that normal people do not have ... and maybe never can have. I had to remind myself that he was just a kid my age. And all of us kids living an itinerant carnival existence lived our lives in fast-forward.

"What happened after you returned from the river, Croak?"

"As soon as I got back to the church shelter, the priest informed me that my mother died. The timing was so bad that at first, I didn't believe him. I called him a 'lying Beelzebub,' which was the first thing that popped into my head. Then he sat me down and made me listen to the heartbreaking truth. The strange part is that she died right around the time I nearly drowned. To me, that was not only bizarre but also mystical.

"'Your mother has finally found her freedom,' the priest said with one of those facial expressions that implies, *I'm supposed to act concerned, but I'm much more interested in that piece of lint on my robe*. When I asked him, what she was free of, he answered, 'freedom from the confines of her grotesque body.' It was as if he didn't even see me standing in front of him in my own dwarf body."

"Oh, Croak!"

"Something happened to me that was akin to a rifle kickback. I decided I wanted to live. I wanted to prove to him that someone of my shape and stature had just as much right to be on the planet as he did. 'You're the person confined. You're trapped in a mind molded by preconceived ideas about what's normal and beautiful. *My* freedom is one of acceptance. Your life is limited by a fear of what's different. You're nothing but a pious, wine-swilling coward in a girly-man dress.' I'm not sure why I added the last part. I guess I was just on a roll, but it sure made me feel good."

"It makes me feel good to hear it," I laughed. "So how did you meet Jones?"

"I said a last goodbye to my mother, and before they could turn me over to the orphan squad, I ran away. The carnival was set up near our town, so I just walked in and asked for the show owner. Jones knows how old I am now, but at the time he didn't. Because I'm a dwarf with an odd voice, people can't figure out how old I am, so I wasn't afraid of passing as legal age. 'I'm looking for work,' I told him. 'I'll work hard, but I need to be in a place where people recognize I have value.'

"I'll never forget what Jones told me. He said, 'I will value you as a person, son, and it's up to you whether you want to join the freak show. The people in my show with physical oddities choose to show off their uniqueness, but they are not expected to. The choice is yours. If you don't want to perform, you can do whatever labor you can handle. We always need extra hands. Here you have freedom of choice. I have others to protect, so promise me you are not a criminal. No other questions asked.'"

Bear sat down at the table next to Croak and draped one arm over his shoulder. "I know Jones has his flaws, but to me, he's practically a saint."

"'Freedom of choice' he told me. Believe it or not, I never knew I had that. I assumed my fate was determined by a body that Mother Nature had failed. And even though I was only fourteen at the time, he inspired me. Now every day I remind myself that here I can be whatever I want to be. I don't have to be a football someone tosses around. I want to be the guy in the top hat."

"We won't ever let anybody do that to you again, Croak," I assured him.

"Thank you both. Only one person here has ever picked me up and swung me around as though I'm some sort of plaything."

"What? Who would do such a thing?"

"Someone who doesn't belong here."

"You're talking about Zee." Bear and I looked at each other in disgust, knowing that Zee was the only bully who might be capable of such cruelty and disrespect.

"He's the person who taunted Sim!" I exclaimed.

"Yes. He's the one poor decision Jones made because Zee showed up when he was short on workers. Please help keep Zee away from me as much as you can. And you need to avoid him too, Rainy. I see the way he looks at you. He's bad news."

31

SOUTHERN VALENTINE

Selfishly speaking, our two weeks of quarantine due to the polio scare were wonderful for me. I was with Bear and Croak a majority of every day; and because the show was shut down, we weren't working much, so we were basically on vacation.

Although I kept my feelings about Bear to myself, I felt closer to him every day, despite our 3 1/2 year age gap. Melba told me I had grown up quickly during the two years since Gramps and I first arrived. I suppose that was one positive effect of our complicated situation and unorthodox lifestyle. Travel was also a source of growth and change, and I learned to adapt quickly to whatever circumstances life brought our way.

Croak and I seemed to have the same outlook on life. Few people our age outside the carny world had separate living quarters, so we felt independent and older than our years. We didn't think like teens, yet we weren't adults. As Croak jokingly quipped, we were "ta-dults."

Although Croak lived in a shared car with Joel, the new ride jock, he was self-sufficient. He painted his side of the divided wagon royal blue and gold, fashioned a throne out of a rocking chair, and declared himself King of the Crappy Cubicle.

In addition to my time with Bear and Croak, quarantine had other advantages as well. I joined Prim and my grandpa for dinner every day, and it was heartwarming to see how happy they were together. They smiled all the time, which is not something I can say of everyone else.

Grandpa, who was still running the office, confided in me that times were rough for Jones. Gramps tried to get the insurance company to cover some of the bills incurred due to the hurricane damage and the polio shutdown, but all his attempts failed because the insurance company referred to both events as "acts of God." I was as angry and disgusted as Gramps was because I couldn't see God in any of those acts. All I could see was a good man struggling to make ends meet.

It was during that time that Jones, with his usual plucky spirit, reminded Gramps that a business must invest money to make money. Only as Jones put it, "Green out-green in."

Jones hired a Cuban named Samaha who had tattoos and piercings all over his body and was looking for employment and a place to live. A giant who went by the name of "Zeus," also joined the show as a needed replacement for Winston.

We were all sad to hear that Winston would not return. He was a gentle giant who had developed a relationship with the twin boys, only to learn that one would be in leg braces for the rest of his life, while the other was confined to a polio ward indefinitely. Gramps said that Jones, despite his recent financial setbacks, sent Winston a large severance bonus to help cover medical bills.

Fortunately, no one else contracted polio, so at the beginning of November, as soon as our quarantine was lifted, we jumped to our next location in Savannah, Georgia. Jones loved Savannah, so he had booked us for a four-week stint, which was twice as long as we were accustomed to being in one location.

Bear, who researched and wrote an article about every city we visited and had recently sold a few essays to local magazines, had visited Savannah several times. He described the historical city as, "quintessentially southern and romantic." I had visions of mossy trees, horse-drawn carriages, cobblestone streets, and antebellum homes. It was all of that and more.

Unfortunately, it was also the setting for one of the most tumultuous months of my life since becoming a fugitive.

Valentine. That's the name the new exotic dancer went by-- simply Valentine. Even her name was beautiful. At twenty-three, she was six and a half years older than I was, so next to her, I felt like a geeky kid. Although she was younger than Esther, our German sword swallower, she was every bit as glamorous.

When Valentine first walked onto the grounds, she sucked the sound out of the air. I was standing with Bear and Melba near one of the concession stands when she approached us to inquire about the location of the office.

"You're looking for work here?" Bear asked.

Even if my severed head were stuffed and mounted for display at the Smithsonian Institute, it would have been impossible for me not to notice Bear's interest in her. I never had to share him with another woman before, so the feelings I instantly experienced were foreign to me. Valentine was so electric that even Melba and I were captivated.

Valentine was gregarious and forthcoming as she lingered to explain her intentions. She ran her hand through her long black hair, her red nails peeking through like decorations on a

Christmas tree. "I'm Valentine, and I'm looking for your boss because I just left my husband. That contemptible coward hit me for the last time." She pointed to a faint bruise near her eye, but all I could see was a row of dark lashes and flawless ivory skin.

"I was employed at a dance hall, but I'm hoping to work with a traveling show so I can make money with y'all and leave Savannah behind."

"The business office is over there in that green Bedford truck," Bear pointed. "The boss's name is Jones. We always need dancers, so I'm sure he'll be thrilled to have you."

Valentine looked Bear up and down and smiled. "I hope you'll be happy to have me too."

She spoke to him sweetly, rather than in a flirtatious manner, but her southern drawl made every word sound like an invitation to her bedroom.

"We will all be happy to have you, Miss, uh--"

"Just 'Valentine,' like the heart."

"I'm Bear. I'm the talker who introduces all the dancers. You and I will be working together if you join the show. This is Rainy and that's Melba."

Bear flashed her one of his Ipana Toothpaste smiles, which made me want to kick him in his teeth. I had an urge to kick Valentine too, but then she completely upended my emotions.

"Boy, you sure are beautiful!" she told me. Her compliment came right out of the blue. "I would love to have platinum hair like yours. And look at that perfect nose and those huge blue eyes. I am just so envious! Can you dance?"

"I, uh, uh ..."

"Dance?" Bear laughed. "She can't even talk!"

As soon as he noticed my discomfort, he realized he had embarrassed me. Bear was oblivious sometimes, but he was never unkind. "I'm sorry," he said directly to me before turning back to Valentine. "Rainy is my best friend. And I agree with you--she's gorgeous. She is very special."

"Indeed, she is!"

I stood in silence, not knowing how to respond. Although I loved being Bear's best friend, I wanted to be more than that to him. At the same time, I was elated by his words. The realization that Valentine had kindly and skillfully directed his focus back to me squelched my desire to hit them both in the face with a shovel.

"If I get hired on, maybe you can give me tips on how to get my hair so shiny, Rainy. Even your name is intriguing! It's so nice to meet y'all."

Melba, Bear, and I stood in silence as Valentine headed toward the office. For a moment, we bobbed in her wake until Melba finally blurted what we were all thinking, "Wow! That gal gives off so much heat she could roast a turkey."

We broke into laughter, which filled the vacuum Valentine left when she departed. I couldn't help but notice how Bear's eyes lingered on her backside as she walked away. Even her backside had a drawl.

I wondered if Bear ever stared at me when I turned my back on him to leave. Sometimes I caught him looking at me, but I never knew what he was thinking. All I knew was that I couldn't walk like Valentine did. She made walking an art form.

Suddenly, I realized that for the first time in my life, I was jealous. Worse yet, I was jealous of someone who had been very kind to me, which seemed so unfair. It was a dark and uncomfortable emotion accompanied by a heavy sense of shame.

I was angry at Bear for noticing her beauty (which a person in a coma couldn't miss), and I was angry with myself for being dressed in work clothes, and sputtering like an idiot, and for

being only sixteen. I was even miffed at Melba, who was inno-
cently standing by with a serene expression on her face while
my ricocheting emotions were searching for a place to light. I
couldn't make sense of it all.

An interloper had sneaked into my cloistered world, and I
was inexplicably threatened. And yet, what was even more
confusing was that a part of my muddled brain hoped Jones
would let Valentine sign on with the carnival. I wanted a
female friend who was close enough to my age to share the fun
activities other young women enjoy.

Hungry to learn about women's issues, and even more
about the outside world, I had visions of sleepovers, gossip,
manicures, and all the other things I had missed out on for
more than two years. I wanted to discuss the latest fashions,
play records, trade movie magazines, and participate in the
pastimes I imagined Margie White and my former school
chums doing without me. And I needed to talk to girls about
our male counterparts.

Despite a fling with a local college student in Charleston
who was doing roustie work as summer employment, I had
only limited experience with the opposite sex. And no
romantic encounters had ever diminished my feelings for Bear.
Even though I usually tried to hide my feelings, I longed to tell
someone about him.

Despite those desires, I was also filled with mental images
of Bear falling in love with someone like Valentine who was
older, more sophisticated, and impossibly sexy. I felt him slipping away from me, even though he was never mine.

Something felt different, but those concerns were mine to
deal with alone. How could I ever tell Bear that at night I
dreamed of the day when he would embrace me again the way
he held and protected me during the hurricane?

I was just his coworker and his buddy. I was too familiar,

too young, and too inexperienced. Bear loved stories, and Valentine had a story to tell. I was just Rainy, the girl with a false surname and no past that I could share. The person I was couldn't possibly be enough.

"I bet she's an excellent dancer," Bear said as Valentine disappeared into the office.

"You're an idiot," I sneered. I remained very calm and upright as I turned my back on him, leaving him standing there with a confused expression on his face. It took all my pride and resolve not to cry, but I kept walking.

32

SAVANNAH TRANQUILIZER

Although I had so many mixed emotions about Valentine, I loved hearing Primrose tell the story of how she was hired. It was especially funny because she recounted the details in front of my grandfather.

"I brought your grandfather lunch, so I was in the office when the dear girl slinked in. Your grandfather was the first person to notice her, and he immediately coughed because his breathing was somehow impeded. I couldn't breathe either because I was trying so hard not to laugh."

"That wasn't a cough, my dear. I had something in my throat."

"Yes, Reese, it's called a gulp. You gulped like a big ol' mackerel. That was just before you nearly succumbed to a fit of hiccups."

"That happens to me a lot around lunchtime."

"You hadn't even eaten your lunch yet, my love. You were a symphony of spasms." Prim's body was shaking like jelly, her chest undulating like a roller coaster, which made us all laugh even harder.

"Very funny, you two comedians," Gramps grinned sheepishly, "I confess to losing my composure a wee bit. But I wasn't as bad as Jones."

"That's a low bar to set," Prim teased. "But you're right. Jones was so stunned when he saw her that as he stood up, he slammed his knee against his open desk drawer. It was painful to watch him stifle a scream. Then he removed his hat, which he seldom does, you know. But when he remembered he was bald, he slapped it back on his shiny dome. Sadly, the hat had turned inside out, so it squatted on his head like a chicken ready to roost."

"Oh, how embarrassing!"

"Not exactly, because Valentine told him he didn't need a hat. 'You have a lovely shaped head, Mr. Jones,' she oozed in that breathy voice of hers. The poor guy was so flustered he forgot all about his hat. It just perched there as if ready to hatch a few eggs."

"I wish I had been there. Tell me more!"

"It was painful to watch." Prim and Grandpa were laughing so hard that Prim could hardly spit out the rest of the story. "Jones set his coffee on his chair while he rifled through his stack of papers to find the employment forms. After he handed them to her, he said he'd be happy to show her around the show. He then promptly sat down on top of his coffee cup."

"Oh n-o-o! What did he do?"

"We'll never know. By then, Reese and I were losing our composure, so we had to leave the office. But apparently, Jones hired her on the spot. And I'm happy to report that your Grandfather managed to exit without walking into a wall, thus retaining what remained of his dignity."

"I take the Fifth, but everything she said about Jones is true," Gramps joked. "Later, I asked him why he didn't have her dance as an audition, and he said, 'She likes my head,

Reese. That's all I need to know.'" By then, even Gramps was in tears from laughing.

"But what if she can't dance?"

"I asked the same thing, and Jones said, "'Oh, hell, Reese, the men in the audience will pay extra money just to follow her inside the tent. And once they do, I don't care if she collapses in the corner like a piece of furniture. She'd make a lovely sofa.'"

———

Valentine had been there a while before she was scheduled for her first show. She was friendly to everybody, which interfered with my efforts to avoid developing a fondness for her.

I remember once asking Melba how she could be so patient with the pinheads, who were often very mischievous. I'll never forget her answer. "Rainy, have you ever tried to be angry with someone who is always smiling?"

Melba's comment now made more sense. That was my problem with Valentine--she was always smiling. She was so magnetic it was almost painful. My jealous attempts to resist her charm were as futile as the attempts of the male carnies to act nonchalant when she passed by. Prim jokingly noted that Jones needed to increase his accident liability insurance policies for Valentine's distracted male admirers.

On the day Valentine was hired, she went home, packed up her suitcases, and returned via bus. Jones had assigned her Cassie's wagon, which had a beige interior that was as uninspired as Cassie had been.

"Come and help me decorate," she told Melba and me. "We'll have a girls-only tea party."

That afternoon was very exciting. Melba said we should dress up just for fun. I didn't have dress-up clothes, so out of respect for the occasion, I borrowed Croak's top hat. When Valentine saw me, she squealed with delight.

"A top hat—how divine! You are an original, and nothing is better than an original! I bow to your artistic sensibility," she added with a dramatic curtsy. "How 'bout if you pour the tea for your humble admirers?"

Within a short time, the three of us were so relaxed that we couldn't stop giggling. Everything seemed so warm and wonderful that my natural shyness disappeared.

Melba and I told Valentine stories about the carnival and the people who traveled with us. After I acted out a funny story about Croak getting stuck in an outhouse and then popping his head out of the top like Punxsutawney Phil, I reigned myself in. "Oops, I am afraid I'm talking too much."

"Not at all! I'm glad the vodka tea relaxed you. I call it a Savannah Tranquilizer. Keep talking. I could listen to your stories all day!"

"Vodka? I've never had alcohol before!"

"You'll never be able to say that again, girl," Melba laughed. "Tell us another story while you top off my tea. Tranquilize me real good, Rainy. Whoopee!"

We had a glorious time decorating the wagon with interesting fabrics and knickknacks that Melba had brought over from her wagon. When Valentine finally started unpacking, I noticed how sexy all her garments were. Her sleepwear was especially feminine, unlike mine, which was more appropriate for a prizefighter.

Lookie here! I didn't even realize I threw this in my bag," she exclaimed. This is not my color, but it would look great on you, Rainy. Can you use it?"

I was stunned when she placed a butter-yellow Angora wool sweater in my hands. Never in my life had I owned anything so fine. I pressed the soft sweater against my face and smiled. I was too thrilled to say much more than, "Thank you, Valentine."

"Melba, I don't want you to think I'm forgetting you, dear, because you also deserve finery. But you're so thin that I worry about you getting cold easily, so I want you to have this soft, flowered shawl. It's from Mexico. I think it's cheerful, don't you?"

"I don't know what to say, Valentine."

"Just say you'll take it and that you'll never get cold. We girls have to take good care of each other, right? Who else do we have?"

"Didn't your husband take care of you, Valentine?"

"No, Max just wanted to control me. Some men are good, Rainy, and some men are not. Your grandpa is a good one. Pick one like him."

"Melba had a husband, but I've never been with a man."

"That time will come, honey," Melba said.

"Melba is right. Just remember that you should be the one to do the picking. Don't give yourself to somebody because he chooses you. That's what I did wrong. But that's all behind me. Now let's turn on some music and dance. I'm going to teach you two how to shimmy, and then let's paint our nails."

That afternoon, I found another bundle of Christmas.

33

SHOWTIME

Everyone was looking forward to Valentine's first performance. Especially the men, of course. Melba and I had already seen her dance in her wagon, and she danced as gracefully as she walked. She was seductive, but she wasn't crass in any way.

"Men are so easy to please and even easier to fool," she told us. "I strip down to a bikini and cover myself with fans, accentuating the feminine mystique. Then I move the fans slowly over my body, teasing them with a promise of getting a glimpse of something more. Suggestion is such a powerful tool."

When it was time for Valentine to go on stage, Melba, Prim, Gramps, and I all made it a point to be there. Bear was training a new talker who had introduced the freak show. The freaks were always a draw, so a huge crowd had accumulated around the bally stage to hear about the next act.

When Bear stepped out on stage, I was as thrilled to see him as I always was. He looked very handsome, and he was more dressed up than usual. Bear stepped to the edge of the bally stage and took a dramatic pause before looking down at the audience and saying, "I hope you're prepared for this, gentleman. We respectfully ask anyone with a health problem to leave now."

Bear waited for a beat before continuing the buildup. "The women I'm about to bring out on stage will stop your heart. And if you have your woman with you, she might catch you drooling and kill you in your sleep. Don't say you weren't warned!"

After the laughter died down, Bear moved to a position farther back on stage, and then, one by one, he called the dancers out for the tease. All the ladies were very attractive, but Valentine had no equal. She was younger and more beautiful than the others, so Bear saved her until the end. When she finally stepped out onto the stage in a white sequined cloak, she dazzled under the lights.

"Gentlemen, I hear you murmuring," Bear winked as he pointed to several men in the audience. "And I know what you're thinking: 'This woman is the most beautiful woman I've ever seen!' Well, tonight your dreams are about to come true, my friends, because if you pay a little extra to go inside the tent, you will see even more of her."

Valentine let one shoulder of her cloak slip down to chest level as she smiled coquettishly at the audience. Slowly, she turned her back to the audience and allowed the cloak to slip even further down to her waist, revealing a naked back. As she turned again to face the crowd, she lifted the cloak to her breasts just in time to avoid exposure.

Prim whispered to Melba and me that Valentine was wearing a skin color bikini, but it was a convincing suggestion of nudity. Bear was staring also, and when he turned back to the audience, he shook his head as if he were trying to avoid passing out. The audience cheered in response to his antics.

"She is a goddess whose movements will soothe you, and

whose gestures will stroke you. We call her Valentine because she will steal your heart." Once again, Valentine slid her garment down just enough to promise more. Bear ogled Valentine again before he sauntered over to her. He lifted her cloak and stroked her bare shoulder with the back of his hand, and then he brushed her hair aside before tucking the garment around her. He then blew on his fingers as though they were scorched.

The way Bear touched her made me so uncomfortable I wanted to run back to my wagon. Sensing my anxiety, Melba placed her hand on my arm and whispered, "It's part of the show, Rainy. It's all an act. He wants the other men to identify with him so they will enter the tent. And they will. That's what makes him so good."

Melba was right. As soon as Valentine disappeared backstage, the men started pushing to get up onto the bally stage where they could pay extra money to go behind the curtain.

"Bear was very good tonight," Prim said. "He's a true showman."

I was contemplating how much was 'show' and how much was 'man,' when I heard a string of shouts accompanied by an alarming commotion.

———

"Valentine!" a loud voice yelled over the crowd. Suddenly a man I didn't recognize jumped up onto the bally stage and stomped toward the curtain. "Either you come out here now or I'm coming back there to get you. We can play this any way you choose, but you're coming home with me. Get out here now, Valentine!"

Valentine peered out from behind the curtain, and when she saw the man, she screamed. "I'm not going home with you,

Max. Go away! I told you it's over. I never want to see you again. You need to leave me alone."

"You're my wife. I ain't never gonna leave you alone."

The man prowled the stage like a lion hunting his prey. Then, with one sudden move, Max reached his arm through the opening in the curtain and grabbed Valentine by the hair, yanking her out onto the stage. In full view of the audience, he smacked her hard across the cheek. He then tried to pull her off the stage, but within seconds, Bear was on top of him. As he wrestled Max to the floor, Valentine ran for safety.

Many people in the crowd were screaming, while others were backing away. I was in shock as I watched Bear rolling around on the stage with Max. To everyone's horror, Max bit Bear's ear and then punched him in the groin, knocking the breath out of him.

Max then stood up and loomed over Bear. He wiped Bear's blood off his mouth, and then he furtively reached into one pocket.

"He's got a knife!" Someone in the audience yelled.

Bear jumped to his feet. There was a flash of knife blade just before Max went after Bear, who quickly sidestepped him. But in doing so, Bear lost his balance and went down again. "I'll kill you," Max raged. He made a hulking gesture toward Bear like a wild animal stalking prey.

Gramps and I were running toward the stage when, seemingly out of nowhere, another figure rushed the stage. He hurled his body at the back of Max's knees, taking him down in one fell swoop. When Max rolled onto his back and thrust the knife upward, the man kicked it from his hand and then stomped on Max's arm. He held the arm in place with one booted foot.

Bear got to his feet just as Bugg arrived with a rope to tie

Max's hands. Max continued to struggle, requiring all three of them to restrain him.

During the fight, they ended up at the back of the stage area beyond the spotlights, so I couldn't see the face of the man who stopped the fight. He stood there in silhouette, with only his feet illuminated by the moonlight. When I finally realized who it was, I gasped. The silver-tipped boots belonged to Zee.

34

KISS ME, TONY

Valentine never performed with the show. After the melee on stage, the show was shut down for the evening while the amusement rides remained active. The next day, Valentine told Jones she was leaving.

Gramps was in the office when she gave Jones the news. I hadn't seen Valentine since Melba and I calmed her down after the altercation and accompanied her to her wagon. Therefore, it was a surprise to me when Gramps and I met at lunch, and he told me Valentine was quitting. At my urging, he repeated their conversation.

"She told Jones she never meant to bring her troubles to his doorstep. She was crying so hard, Rainy. It broke my heart. Jones told her that everybody here has troubles, and we're all running from something, even those of us who don't know it."

"He's right, Gramps, we're running too. Couldn't he convince her to stay?"

"No. She told him there was nowhere for her to run. She knows her ex-husband will be back. Although Jones did some checking and found out the thug would be in jail awhile, that information was not enough to reassure her. She insisted that he will never leave her alone. She doesn't want to put us all in that kind of jeopardy."

"Where will she go?"

"I'm not sure, Rainy. She wouldn't say. She's packing up her belongings right now."

I immediately ran to the trailer where Valentine was staying and burst in without knocking. She was bent over a suitcase when I walked in, and when she spun around, she was wielding a hammer. "Oh Rainy, thank heavens it's you!" She exhaled as she set down the hammer.

"Oh my God! I'm so sorry to startle you. I just can't believe you're leaving! Where will you go?"

"Far away from here, love."

"That's not necessary! Jones can assign some rousties as your bodyguards. They can protect you better than anybody else out there. We were just becoming friends, Valentine. I love having you here. Please reconsider."

"We *are* friends, dearest Rainy, but Max has left me no choice. I've been through this with him before. He thinks I'm his property and he will never stop pursuing me. My best protection is to disappear, and I figured out a way to do that. There is someone at a shelter I went to in the past who can help me vanish. That's the only way this will ever stop."

"But he's stealing your life from you!"

"That happened the day I met him. At least he hasn't yet taken my life. But I'll start anew. I'll drink lots of Southern Tranquilizer tea and I'll get a Golden Retriever and a new name. Maybe I'll call myself Rainy. It's such a lovely name," she smiled wistfully.

"Oh, Valentine! Does that mean we'll never see you again?"

"I'm afraid so, honey. Now you must leave me to pack. I don't want to start crying. This is already hard enough. You take care of yourself, you marvelous, magical creature. You must thank Bear for me, and give my love to Melba. I wish we could all be friends forever."

―――――

I went back to my wagon and sobbed. In the brief time I had spent with Valentine, I rediscovered something I had concealed along with my identity. It was the part of me that was feminine and passionate.

For two years, I had been in hiding, and hiding is a lie. Repressing my spirit had become part of the lie, and now, Valentine would experience that same loss of self. I was heartsick for her. We were both among the missing, but at least I had a family, and I would be free when I reached eighteen. Valentine would be a prisoner of the lie forever.

―――――

As I lay on my bed, the bright orange and black monarch butterflies Croak and I had constructed from paper and strung along one wall of my wagon seemed to be flying upward toward the sky-color ceiling as if looking for a means of escape. Like the monarchs, I wanted to fly away too.

I was losing my friend, someone who had reminded me that I was no longer a girl, but a near-woman with desires and deep emotions. However, as I stared at the constellation of neon stars glued to the ceiling, I realized I was just a speck in the universe, and my problems were even smaller by comparison, no matter how big they often seemed. I would be free one day soon, but Valentine was the butterfly who could never escape.

After I blew my nose and finally pulled myself together, I

realized I was late for my work shift. Melba was now cleaning ride cars with Zee because she knew how uncomfortable he made me. My job was to clean the school trailer, which was a labor of love.

After I dried my eyes, I shoved my hair under a baseball cap as I usually did and reached for my sunglasses. As soon as I opened the door, I was face-to-face with Bear.

"I've been standing out here, Rainy. I heard you crying, and I didn't know whether to knock or go away."

Bear stepped up the three stairs to the wagon and gently shoved me back inside. "You can't go to work like this. Croak is already there cleaning up, so I think you should just stay here and relax. Com'on, let's sit down."

When we went back inside, I sat on the bed while Bear took a seat in the overstuffed chair opposite me.

"How is your ear?

"Sore, but it will heal. I hope he had his rabies vaccination."

"Your face is bruised too. Can I offer you--"

"Forget the formalities, Rainy. It's only me, remember? Can we talk about your tears, please? I haven't been able to figure out exactly what's going on with you because I'm nothing but a dumb guy, but I am not so thick that I can't see that your sadness is about much more than Valentine's departure."

"She was so nice to me, Bear. And even though she was older than I am, she was closer to my age than Melba and Prim."

"I can understand that. She was very kind, and we will all miss her."

"Yes, I realize you will miss her too. I know you thought she was special."

"That's true. She was very special. I said goodbye to her a few minutes ago. She just left. I'm sorry, Rainy."

"Me, too, Bear. Do you think maybe you would have had a chance with her if she stayed?"

"A chance to do what? To be friends? Of course!"

"I think you know what I mean. I saw how you looked at her, and I don't blame you. Every man in this place was overwhelmed by her."

"Yes, I thought she was beautiful. I'm not blind and I'm not dead. But I wasn't overwhelmed, to use your word, Rainy. Valentine was a sweet gal, but I like women who are a little more cerebral. Besides, she was too old for me and too advanced, so anything more than friendship was not something I would ever have considered."

"Too old? She was three years older than you, and you're three years older than me. And you're advanced in lots of areas. So what does that mean?"

"Rainy, I am not as experienced as you seem to think. Just like you, I joined the carnival when I was a teenager, so I have had most of the same experiences and limitations you've had. In some ways, I'm still just a kid. Sure, I've fooled around a bit in all my travels--I'm not gonna deny that--but I've never had a steady girlfriend before. At least not a real one."

"But you had a fake one?" I grinned.

"Now, there's the smart-talkin' Rainy we all know! For a moment there, I thought you had disappeared on me. It's nice to see you smiling again. And yes, I do have a fake girlfriend. The poor thing is a bit of a wooden head, though."

"Are you referring to that marionette Croak carved for you? Matilda? I've seen you dancing around your wagon with her. It's creepy but very touching."

"Stop laughing. Matilda is very sexy when she does the tango. And I'm glad you think my taste in wood puppets is so hilarious. But, sadly, my blockhead girlfriend hasn't been able to figure out that I love her."

"Wait a minute, are we still talking about somebody fake?"

"Fake identity, but that's out of necessity. And I've been hesitant to tell her I'm in love with her because if I do, her feisty grandfather might beat the stuffing out of me."

Although I was momentarily speechless, I didn't need to hear any more words than that. I ran across the room and flung myself into his lap. "You better be talking about me," I said, "or I'm gonna feel like a dang fool."

"You're the gal I'm talking about, although Matilda is stiff competition. Can you tango?"

"I'll learn!"

"So, Lorraine Merrill, are you going to let me kiss you?"

I jerked my head back and then immediately stood up and backed away from him. "What did you just call me?"

"I called you by your name, Rainy. I'm so sorry. It was just spontaneous. But I will never say it aloud in public."

"How long have you known?"

"More than a year."

"But how did you find out?" Hearing my name was foreign and frightening. I felt as though I had been stripped naked. My heart was pounding as I dropped onto the bed and stared at him.

"I write articles about every town we set up in, remember? And every time we are in Endicott, you and your grandfather seem to disappear. Jones adjusts your work schedules, and you never go into town to explore like you do when we are in other locations. It wasn't hard to figure out that Endicott was a problem for you."

"But you know my name."

"Yes, I came upon it by accident. When I researched the area at the local library, I found some articles about your disappearance. Once I made the connection, I decided not to write the article. I would never hurt you."

"Do you believe my grandpa abducted me?"

"Absolutely not! But I think you need to continue to do everything possible to hide your identity. I was a product of the foster system, remember? I don't want that for you, Rainy. You mustn't relax until you are free."

"In a year and a half, I'll be of legal age, and we've been safe here for more than two years.

"But you can't let down your vigil. I don't think you are as careful as you believe you are."

"What do you mean?"

"That framed photo on your bookcase of your mother and father--when you showed it to me, I noticed their names on the back. It's easy to slip up, Rainy. As I told you before, people like Zee cannot be trusted."

"But I thought maybe we had misjudged him. He saved your life, Bear."

"Yes, he did, and I'm grateful for that. He's a darn good fighter, and I told him so. But just because someone is a good fighter, that doesn't make him a good man. He has been asking me and others a lot of questions about you."

"Like what?"

"He asked me what Rainy was short for, so to throw him off, I told him it was just a funny nickname we gave you because your real name is Stormy."

"Stormy? That sounds like a stripper."

"I had to think fast."

"I'm surprised you didn't say that my name is Tony."

"I'm glad to see you still have your sense of humor. But I'm serious, Rainy. He also asked how old you are, so I said you're eighteen, and I stuck with the standard line that you're from New Jersey, but I don't think he bought it."

"Yikes. I think I better learn something about New Jersey

that doesn't involve spaghetti and Frank Sinatra. So, why do you think Zee was asking about me?"

"At first, I thought he had a crush on you."

"That's a disgusting thought. He's twice my age, Bear!"

"Yes, but smarmy men like Zee don't have any boundaries. That's something I learned when hitchhiking across the country. I'm not sure what Zee's motivation is, but I want you to be extra careful, even though I will be looking out for you as always."

"I'm so glad you're here, but why have you never left, Bear? Don't you feel confined?

"Not at all. Why would I want to leave? I have a home, a fun job, interesting friends, free education, and I travel all the time. That's more than I could ask for with almost any other job or lifestyle."

"You don't have dreams for something bigger?"

"Bigger? It's not that my dreams aren't big enough, Rainy-- it's that I'm fulfilled. This is a darn big stage we live on. You feel trapped because of your situation, and understandably so. But I can leave at any time, and whenever I do, I always look forward to coming home."

"Does this feel like a permanent home to you?"

"Yes, it does. My railroad car is an apartment on wheels, which is a unique and appealing dwelling in my book. To some folks, a nomadic lifestyle would be unsettling, but I think it's pretty darn exciting. Every day is full of surprises."

"Well, I certainly cannot argue with that."

"I view my life inside the fence as a privileged existence within a private enclave, whereas it's a cage to you. The difference between us is freedom of choice. I'm so sorry you're in this situation, Rainy. If there weren't strict laws for minors considered to be runaways, you could live anywhere without being hunted. Then you might see things differently."

"I do love it here, Bear, but you're right, I feel trapped at times."

"I hope the day will come when you no longer feel that way. Please trust that you can just relax and be yourself when we are together. And even though I know about your past, I give you my word here and now that you will always be safe with me."

"Thank you, Bear. It's such a strange feeling to learn that you know the real me."

"Yes, I do know you. And have you forgotten that I finally had the guts to tell you I'm in love with you?"

"I think I remember that," I smiled. "I love you too, Bear Deane.

"Then get back over here and kiss me, Tony."

BOOK III: AIR IN A BOX

35

NEW HOPE, PENNSYLVANIA - 1953

Being in love with Bear was like carrying around a ball of sunshine inside me. I was always warm and bright, and everything around me seemed to reflect that.

I continued to do my chores and go to school, and I spent a lot of time with Primrose and Grandpa. After dinner, we would play cards, and Bugg and Bear would often join us. Prim taught a group of us how to play bridge, so Melba, Croak, Alva, and a new roustie named Brearley sometimes joined us on the one night a week the show was dark.

During our stay in Delaware, we picked up another dancer named Cecelia, and like Prim, she was an excellent singer. During our Sunday services, Gramps played a wonderful selection of tunes as Prim and Cecelia sang along to all the pop hits. Although someone usually wanted to say a quick prayer or recite a verse or poem, the services were not specifically religious. They were entertaining, inspirational, and bonding. Gramps called the get-togethers "a kitchen sink full of socialization."

My new job was helping with laundry and chores for

people like voluptuous Vivian, our two pinheads, and a few others with physical limitations that prevented them from handling their daily routines. I had learned how to be a caretaker with Earl, so it came naturally to me.

We had a new member of the Human Oddity attraction named Flipper Man, whom we called 'Flip.' He had been born with wing-like appendages instead of arms, and he had only one partially-formed leg. I was in awe of how self-sufficient he was.

One day, while I was in his trailer helping him change his bed, he told me he had been part of the carnival circuit since he was a young boy. "My parents abandoned me in St. Louis in 1925 when I was five years old. Back in those days, if kids like me disappeared, no one even asked questions. Some parents even drowned deformed kids. Hospitals didn't want us, and even convents turned down those of us with the most severe defects because of the amount of care required."

"Where did your parents send you?"

"I was traded to a carnival owner who barely fed me and made me sleep on a hay pile without a blanket. During winter, I had to burrow into the hay to keep from freezing, so a proper bed with a blanket is a true luxury to me."

"I'm happy you have a bed, too, Flip. And I promise you will always have blankets. How did you get here?"

"I convinced a ride jock in my former outfit to bring me to New Hope when I heard Jones's show was playing here. It just so happens that my driver is from this area, so when he mentioned he was heading this way to visit his family, I quit my last show and paid him most of my savings to bring me with him. He's a kind chap who assisted me all the way here from Alabama. Joining this show has been my goal for years."

"It has?"

"Sure! On the carnival circuit, this outfit is known for its fair treatment of freaks like me."

"To be honest with you, Flip, I have always been very uncomfortable with the word 'freak.'"

"Most of us freaks accept the term, Rainy. It wasn't always so offensive, because it just meant that we were unusual. And we are. But as showmen started treating us as though we were animals, the word became associated with something hideous. I think that's why good people like Jones use the word 'oddity' to denote that we are unusual. And we all know that we are. But I think 'work of art' is a more accurate description, don't you? And wouldn't Picasso agree?" he winked.

"Well, I certainly agree! But how do you feel about being on display in a show?"

"It's the only life I know. My entire existence is a display. And where would I be without a freak show? I would be in an institution somewhere. Or even dead. But at least I now have a good employment situation, a paycheck, food, and a place to live. I feel fortunate to be here. Jones is famous among our lot for being a kind man."

"He has always been good to me too."

"He's trapped in an unusual body himself, which probably makes him more compassionate. He's a funny fella, and so easy-going."

"But I should warn you that he sure can be stubborn," I laughed. "Once he banned hotdogs for three months because he thought they were giving everyone too much gas. We all complained, but he didn't relent until several rousties took Whoopie cushions to the lunch table to make a point. He is eccentric, but he always tries to keep his carnies happy."

I thought about how Jones had changed my work assignment after Melba recommended I work with someone other than

Zee. I was very grateful, especially because Melba was the person who was stuck with cleaning the amusement ride cars with Zee. However, she had figured out how to keep a distance from him. Rather than two people working on one car as she and I did, she had him clean the even-numbered red cars while she took the others. She told me she relished the silence between them.

According to Melba, Zee slacked off a lot by stopping for endless cigarette breaks or simply lounging around. She was concerned he wasn't thoroughly inspecting the cars for damage and planned to have a conversation about it with Jones.

Zee was up to his old habits of following me to the school trailer, and he often appeared out of nowhere when I was picking up food at the cookhouse for the people I assisted. I didn't want to complain to Jones, because Zee kept his distance and didn't exactly do anything I could report as being out of line. He was just *there*.

Zee always startled me and made me feel quite uncomfortable, and although I was relieved not to be spending my work hours with him, I was always apprehensive about running into him. There was some talk that he might leave the show soon, so I prayed that our stay in New Hope would be his last stop.

I learned that even the most sincere prayers often go unanswered.

36

THE SQUEEZE

Whenever we were in a new town, I continued to go on excursions with Gramps, but now Prim and Bear often joined us. When I first asked Gramps if Bear could tag along with us, I explained that he and I had become good friends. "Uh-huh, 'friends,'" Gramps repeated.

"Why do you have that goofy look on your face?"

"What look? I don't know what you're talking about. No one with two brain cells would ever question that you and Bear are 'friends.' Just like Rick and Ilsa in 'Casablanca.' They will always have Paris, and you and Bear will always have Savannah." He tried to stifle a chuckle, but Gramps was never very good at subtlety.

"Oh, stop being so corny! Do you think everybody knows?"

"Sweetheart, we all knew before you did!"

"Am I that transparent?"

"To me, you are. But I remember when you preferred measles to boys, so I've had the honor of witnessing the changes."

"Yeah, I remember those days," I smiled. "But Gramps,

there's something you should know. Bear was doing research for his writing while he was in Endicott, and he found out about our past. He knows our real names."

For a moment, Grandpa was silent. Then he looked at me with a deadpan expression and said, "Well, this sure is a baking soda and vinegar set of circumstances."

"Yeah," I smiled at his ironic sense of humor. "I guess it's not the outcome we planned for, Mr. Wizard."

"No, but I've been expecting this day would come. If he found out that easily, that is truly worrisome. Is Bear trustworthy?"

"Yes, he is. Just like Prim and Jones. I think they are the only ones who know the details. But Bugg and Melba also know a lot because they were there from the beginning, and they saw the flyers, remember?"

"Yes, of course. Secrets eventually slip out. Keeping secrets is like trying to keep the air in a box. But we just need a little more time to get through this, Rainy."

"We should be fine, Gramps. We both look much different from how we looked two years ago."

"Yes, of course. And there's no sense fretting about it because you can't put milk back into a cow. So let's hope for the best and go explore New Hope." Gramps put on a cheerful face, but I knew he was troubled.

————

Our day in New Hope was extra special. Usually, the carnies billed as freaks stayed at the show on days off. Not only was it difficult for them to get around, but it was also difficult for them to contend with public interactions that resulted in humiliating situations.

However, Bear and I convinced Croak to join us, and we

even got Flip to agree to come along. Flip had rarely been in the public eye, but he was desperate to see the world. He warned us that people who saw him usually gasped, a reaction he had grown to expect.

"I guess deformities scare people. I was told that some folks believe it's the curse of Satan, or they project my physical abnormalities upon themselves and can't bear the thought. But this body is all I have, Rainy. As a kid, I used to dream about being handsome like Bear, and I fantasized about being able to play baseball like Mickey Mantle. I could never throw a ball, so I taught myself how to hold pastel pens with my right limb. Now I dream of being Toulouse Lautrec. He had physical challenges too, but he was a wonderful artist."

"I love your spirit, Flip, and I think your drawings are amazing. Have you ever been to an art gallery?"

"I've seldom been anywhere beyond carnival grounds. That's why I'm so excited about joining you today in New Hope. And don't worry about me, because I am prepared to face any ugliness that comes my way."

"Do people often harass you?"

"Oh, yes. On my journey to hook up with our show, my traveling companion and I entered a Howard Johnson's road-side restaurant where a brazen woman made a terrible scene when she yelled at my buddy. She told him he had no right to bring someone as frightful-looking as me into a public place where I could scare people and ruin everyone's appetite. Then she called for the manager to kick us out."

"Oh, my God, Flip! What did your friend do?"

"He yelled right back in her face, 'Nobody could ruin an appetite more than you do, lady!' The good part of the story is that the restaurant manager refused to serve her, but we left without eating to avoid another scene."

"Flip, I have no words to tell you how sorry I am, but we are going to have a pleasant lunch today, I promise. I'll help you eat, and we will all protect you."

It required a bit of planning regarding how to best transport Flip. Rather than carry him all afternoon, Bear and Gramps decided to push him in one of Reno's grocery carts because it was more elevated than the Radio Flyer wagon we used to pull him around carnival grounds. After Croak added some pillows as padding, we were ready to go.

———

New Hope is a beautiful town on the Delaware River, and we were all very excited to explore it. The quaint town, which is over 200 years old, is built on a canal with four remaining original locks. But the best part is the thriving Main Street area with all its art galleries and little restaurants that make the area so charming.

Gramps and I had a long-standing tradition that for any excursion, all participants had to read about the town first and then come up with one thing that they wanted to see or do. Bear picked the old restored Lock Tender's house, while I opted for a walk along the canal. Prim had a little bistro in mind that was known for their flaming crêpes and would serve people of her race, which was something we always had to consider. Flip and Croak had both chosen the same art gallery that featured a standing insulation art exhibit on dinosaurs, which was something we were all excited to see.

For a while, the day was everything I had hoped it would be, although it took some time to adjust to people staring at Flip in his cart and at Croak with his unusual frame and disproportionate head sporting a top hat.

The entire time we were there, the more polite people would sneak furtive glances at Flip and Croak before lowering their eyes. In some respects, that was just as bad as staring, because when strangers saw their deformities and quickly turned away, Croak and Flip became invisible, and their humanity seemed to be lost in the pretense of not taking notice. I didn't know whether it was better to be seen as a freak, or not to be seen at all.

As we were waiting for a table at a bistro on Main Street, we were surprised when a man walked up to us, said a friendly greeting to all, and then directed his conversation to Gramps.

"Hello there. Haven't we met?" he asked.

"I don't think so, sir. We're not from these parts."

"Neither am I. I'm from upstate New York, the Triple Cities area. The wife and I are down here for a visit with the kids and I said to her, 'Hey, that guy looks familiar.'" He turned to the queue to give his wife a wave before continuing. "Are you sure you don't recognize me?"

"I'm afraid I don't. But it's lovely chatting with you, and I hope you have an enjoyable afternoon." Gramps silently signaled to us it was time to leave.

"No, wait, please. I'm sure I'm right. You look like the land-scaper who designed the grounds for IBM headquarters in Binghamton, New York. Remember me? I'm Berardi. I'm positive you're the gentleman I used to chat with when I would take my lunch break out on the lawn. You recommended a place called Jukie's in Endicott. It's a dance and music venue, and I believe you said you played there. I think you play piano, right?"

"Oh, how I wish I could, sir. All I can play is opossum. And you seem like a friendly fellow who would be an enjoyable lunch companion, but I'm afraid it must have been someone who looks like me. I am often mistaken for other people. Just once, I would like to be mistaken for Cary Grant instead of one of the Marx Brothers," Gramps said with a nervous laugh.

"But I was sure--"

Suddenly, Bear let out a loud groan, and everyone stopped talking. "I'm sorry to interrupt your conversation, but we have to go home right now," he pleaded. "Please, Pops!"

"Are you okay, son?" Gramps asked.

Bear groaned again and clutched his stomach. "It's that sausage I had for breakfast. I feel so sick that I may vomit. Please, can we go back to the car?"

"Of course! Of course!" Gramps quickly caught on. He grabbed Prim by the arm and spun around to leave.

"Do you have a business card?" the man persisted.

"Sorry, I'm a retired dentist, so I no longer have cards. Nice to meet you, sir," Gramps said over his shoulder. "Have a good day."

As I turned to follow, I noticed a familiar face amongst the line of people who were waiting for a table. The arrogant tilt of the head and the sneering lips belonged to the one person who was an indelible, dark stain in my life. He looked me straight in the face and gave me a conspiratorial look. It was Zee, and he had heard everything. Suddenly, I could feel the walls squeezing in.

37

A LOSS TOO GREAT

It was incongruous to me that as I was just about to turn seventeen, we were back in Endicott once again. We had left New Hope without further incident, but our encounter there made Gramps and me more nervous than ever about being in public.

As soon as we rolled into town, he and I followed our usual routine of lying low. The only work we did was indoors in the business office or in the personal living quarters of one of our carnies who needed physical care. When the carnival was open, we stayed in the employee private area we referred to as the "backyard," never venturing where the public might see us.

Although we had fled from town almost three years earlier, Bear's research had unturned a few newspaper articles about us. According to the papers, Grandpa was still a wanted man.

Neither of us could believe the irony of our situation. Everybody was looking for me, even though I was with my Grandfather who had raised me, yet no one was looking for people like Croak, who was also a minor. And no one had ever looked for Flip when he was a kid, or Sim, either. But their bodies were damaged, so no one made the effort.

Endicott was not the place where I would have wanted my seventeenth birthday to take place. We couldn't venture out into town, but Jones and Reno promised me there would be plenty of ice cream available in the cookhouse. Reno agreed to let Melba use his oven because she wanted to make me her special banana sour cream cake. I knew Flip was working on a chalk drawing for me, but I had no clue what Croak, Bugg, or Bear might be up to. I just knew they would make my birthday special.

Bear and I spent a lot of time alone in my wagon, which we preferred to his. Bear's was very much like my railway car, and just as unique. He had decorated the interior with artificial vines and plants, so it resembled a lush indoor forest. However, his location was far from desirable.

Bear's wagon was situated next to the car where the pinheads, Dotty and Dale, lived with their caretaker, an elderly woman named Gladys. Although we loved the girls, it was hard to be around their nearly uncontrollable energy. They constantly shrieked and squealed, mostly from joy, but the noise was nerve-wracking, so we always ended up at my place.

We shared many intimate moments, and I was becoming closer to being a woman, but most of our time was spent laughing. I loved it when Bear would drape himself in one of my shawls and pretend to be one of our Coochie girls. His dancing was atrocious, but I cheered him on while I imitated him as the self-assured talker he was. I could also do a great imitation of Jones because I had his raspy, cranky voice down to perfection.

Croak, Melba, and some of the ladies usually joined us for the book club that we held on Thursday nights when we read passages from our favorite novels. Gramps and Prim always came too, although they joked about the "exhausting fifteen-step walk" from their door to mine.

Being a Dickens fan, Croak loved to entertain us as Mr. Pickwick from "The Pickwick Papers," but nothing could top his brilliant Miss Havisham characterization from "Great Expectations." For one performance, he showed up in a lace curtain fashioned as a wedding veil, which made us laugh until we were holding our sides. Bear told him his act was worthy of "The Ed Sullivan Show," spurring Croak to launch into his impersonation of Ed Sullivan as a dwarf, which made Melba laugh until she was snorting.

We all found constant ways to entertain each other, so we were sure my party would be memorable. However, no one expected the life-changing events to come.

———

It was a warm August, so Melba decided that my party should be at the picnic tables under the tent in front of the cookhouse. Bear, Prim, and our other friends had gathered early and told me to wait until 8 o'clock to show up. Gramps waited with me because he planned to blindfold me just before we got to the tent so the party décor would be a surprise.

I was full of anticipation as we sneaked along the fence while traversing the area from the private sleeping cars to the outdoor kitchen. As we walked along the fence behind the amusements, we were extra careful to avoid the bright lights that lined the rides like electric snakes.

That night, the carnival was packed with people, their laughter and shouts reverberating through the balmy air. As we passed Big Eli, we could hear screams of thrill mixed with delight as the riders moved higher and higher into the sky. Each time the double wheels of the old Ferris wheel went around, the carts rocked in the breeze.

Grandpa was two steps ahead of me when he stopped in his tracks. He turned around and grabbed my arm and pointed toward the Ferris wheel. "Look up there. Watch the red cart approaching the top. That little girl is slipping out, Rainy!"

When I spotted the cart, I was horrified to see a woman struggling to keep her child from falling out of the Ferris wheel seat. The mother screamed as she tried to get the attention of Joel, the ride jock who was moving the carts one by one to load on new passengers. With all the noise, the woman's screams blended in with all the others.

Joel loaded two more passengers, and turned the gears, sending all the carts even higher.

"She doesn't have a seat strap on!" Gramps cried.

When I looked, I could see that the protruding safety bar was secured across the cart, but the seat strap that was supposed to secure riders in the seat was hanging along the side of the seat in two pieces.

"The strap broke! Someone didn't check the straps," I yelled. "The little girl is slipping out from under the bar, Gramps!"

Grandpa and I immediately started running toward the ride. By the time we reached Big Eli, the mother was holding the little girl by her dress as the child's legs dangled from the cart. They both were screaming as the mother desperately struggled to keep herself and her child from falling out of the cart.

"Shut down the ride, Rainy!" Grandpa told me as he pushed his way through the crowd. "Don't let Joel rotate the carts."

I knew Gramps was right. Each time the carts rotated while loading, there was a rocking motion. We had to bring the ride to a standstill. I ran past Joel into the dog house and shut down the ride as smoothly as I could to minimize the movement. Joel spun around to look at me, an expression of confusion crossing his face.

I ran out of the dog house and pointed to the top of the wheel. "Emergency!" I screamed. When Joel looked up, he gasped in shock.

By then, despite the cacophony of noise around us, the crowds noticed what was happening on the wheel and froze in place. The screaming was no longer from thrill, but from horror as many pointed to the top of the Ferris wheel where the mother had also slipped part-way under the bar while straining to keep a grasp on her child. She was using her legs like scissors to cinch the child to her, but most of their weight was now out of the cart. I knew there was no way she could keep her grip on the safety bar for long.

Suddenly, people were pointing to the lower part of the Ferris wheel frame. When I looked, I could see a man rapidly scaling the support structure, trying to get to the top to save them. It was Grandpa.

There was nothing I could do but watch. He moved quickly and adroitly, climbing higher and higher on the side of the frame closest to the child. A huge crowd had gathered, and rousties were running toward the commotion from other parts of the carnival.

Over my left shoulder, I saw Bugg coming my way. Wordlessly, I pointed to Grandpa who was about three-fourths of the way up the frame. Within seconds, Bugg and our new roustie Brearley were also scaling the frame.

I heard Jones yelling at everyone to stand back as he tried

to clear the area. "Get back for your own safety!" he yelled, but the crowd barely gave way.

Grandpa finally reached the top of the Ferris wheel. He leaned out from the frame and grabbed the little girl with one arm. The child screamed and kicked out of fear, but Grandpa held on. He pulled her into him and yelled something inaudible to the mother, whose body was hanging at an awkward angle from the cart.

Bugg, who was right behind Grandpa, reached up to take the child from his arms. As Grandpa was the highest one on the frame, he then signaled to the woman to let go of the bar and take his hand. She shook her head in terror and refused to let go. Gramps continued to coax her as he reached out farther and farther in her direction.

I held my breath as I watched Gramps swing out from the horizontal bar he was clutching until he could reach her legs and pull her toward him. He guided her feet onto the frame, but by then, she was at an angle, almost perpendicular to the ground. Gramps placed his hands under her waist, and with what seemed to be supernatural strength, he thrust her into a vertical position so she could let go of the cart and grab the frame of the Ferris wheel. Just as she got a grip, Grandpa lost his.

During a heartbeat of time, Grandpa was suspended in space, and then he plunged toward the ground below. I lost my ability to breathe as I watched him fall. My heart plummeted with him to a depth I did not know existed. It only took a few slow-motion moments for the air to swallow him. Then he was gone.

While the frantic crowd screamed and yelled for help, I pushed my way through to the area where Gramps had landed. I could barely comprehend what I was looking at. My Gramps lay on the ground, his arms and legs hideously contorted. As I threw my body on top of him, I suddenly heard Prim next to me screaming his name.

"No!" I screamed. "Gramps, Gramps, wake up! Come back to me! He's bleeding! Someone make him stop bleeding!"

When I slipped my hand under his head, my fingers sunk into a mass of warm tissue. Desperate for help, I looked up at Prim, who stood frozen in place. The gaudy lights distorted her tear-streaked face, cutting into her like shards of glass. Her chest was heaving, as though her heart was trying to climb out of her body.

Bugg was climbing down the wheel with the woman in tow when Bear finally got to the scene. Bear and Jones checked Grandpa for any signs of life, but no one dared speak the truth.

My body shook violently, but the pain and horror were trapped in my throat. I was far removed from my own agonized moans as Bear pulled me into his chest. "Don't look, Rainy," he whispered, "Don't look."

I could hear sirens in the background as Joel covered my grandfather with a blanket from the dog house. Jones announced that the show was closed and ordered everyone to go home. Still, no one moved.

"Someone help her!" Jones yelled as Prim suddenly crumpled to the ground next to Grandpa. "Bring smelling salts!"

Bugg, who was now on the ground safely with the mother and child, ran to where we were standing.

When he saw Grandpa, a look of unspeakable sorrow instantly blanketed his scarred face.

Then he looked at Prim as several people crowded around her. "Air!" he yelled. Before anybody could stop him, he shoved everyone aside and began pounding on Prim's chest. It was only then that we all realized Prim was no longer breathing. We watched in endless horror as Bugg tried to breathe for her.

It only took a few minutes for Prim's heart to decide it

couldn't handle any more shock and pain. By some almost incomprehensible twist of fate, Prim took her last breath. She died next to her husband, my beloved grandfather.

I heard myself scream, and as I sought refuge from the sorrow, I slipped into the comfort of darkness. I closed my eyes, silently begging God to take me with Grandpa and Primrose.

38

THE UNRAVELING

Five days after the accident, we had a small service for Grandpa and Primrose on the carnival grounds. I was still almost paralyzed with shock from watching Gramps and Prim die in such an appalling, ghastly way. I couldn't curtail the horrific images of my grandfather's distorted body--images that ceaselessly threaded through my mind like film through a projector.

How could someone so wonderful be reduced to a lifeless pile of human remains? I had to fight an almost overwhelming urge to claw at my eyes where the images lived to haunt me. How could such a beatific presence suddenly vanish from the earth--and from me?

And Prim was gone too—beautiful Prim, whom I needed to get me through the horror. I had lost another loving mother. How would I ever be happy again without her and Gramps?

Although I was functioning in a near-robotic state, I focused on the memorial service to try to hold the shattered pieces of myself together. Jones and I decided it was best not to conduct the service on the bally stage because that was a place for celebrations and performances, so we all met at the picnic tables under the cookhouse tent, the place where I was supposed to have my birthday party the night Gramps was killed.

There were still streamers hanging from the poles, and when I glanced into a trashcan, I saw a cake with its unburned candles still clinging helplessly to the frosting that had formed a clump on one side of the abandoned cake.

Jones, in his secret and mysterious way, had secured false identification papers for my Grandpa, which the local coroner never questioned. "Charles Whistler" would be buried in a plot in Riverside Cemetery in Endicott, close to the graves of my mother and father.

Prim would be put to rest next to her brother Earl in the same cemetery. It comforted me to know they would all be near each other, and Gramps would never have to look over his shoulder again. He had protected me and sacrificed his life so that I could be with him and be free. Together, we had fought against the odds, and we had made it. Until then. Even with Bear in my life, I wasn't sure I could ever recover from losing my grandfather.

The service was simple. Everybody loved Grandpa and Prim, so many of our friends offered to say a few words. I was too upset to talk, but Bear sang, "You'll Never Walk Alone," which moved everyone to tears.

Jones ended the ceremony by saying, "Gramps was short in stature, but he stood tall as a man. He was soft in heart but strong in fight, he was true and wise, and he was devoted to all that was good. He and our dear Primrose were family, not only to Rainy but to us as well. And he was my hero. Oh, how they will be missed!"

As we walked back to my wagon, Bear sensed my need to be quiet. All he said was, "I will take care of you, Rainy." The pain had formed such a ball in my throat that I couldn't force any words past it, so I squeezed his hand and kept walking.

Together, we sat in my wagon drinking tea. We both knew there would be time to discuss the accident and what we planned to do with Grandpa and Prim's belongings, but first I needed time to gather all the scattered pieces of myself so I could somehow move on.

I stared at a newspaper that was lying face up on my table. Melba brought it to me the day after the accident. Someone in the crowd had taken a picture of Grandpa up on the Ferris wheel as he struggled to save the woman and her child. Somehow, the newspaper acquired the photo and published it on the front page with the headline, "Carny Workers Save Woman and Child." Fortunately, the report said that the workers were unidentified.

The article, which reported a "female carnival employee" suffering a fatal heart attack during the accident, also mentioned that the show was closed while the police looked into the incident. The article called Grandpa a "nameless hero." That made me furious because Gramps had a name until he was forced to give it up. His name was buried with my father, the son the authorities would not recognize as his own.

I was also harboring an unspeakable anger toward Zee. Melba told me he was supposed to clean and inspect the even-numbered Ferris wheel cars--the red ones like the woman and her child were riding in when they nearly lost their lives.

Jones examined the car once they brought it down and determined that the seat buckle had come loose from the strap, something that should have been noticed.

In my mind, there was no question that Zee was responsible for what had happened. It was his careless, arrogant, and lazy nature that caused the accident that ended with the horrific deaths of my grandfather and Prim. I couldn't prove it, but I knew it was true. And I hated him for what he had done.

———

Not only were two people dead, but the carnival was in a world of trouble. Jones told everybody to pack up and be ready to leave once the police department permitted us to move on. In the meantime, most of us either stayed in our trailers or drank coffee and played cards on the picnic tables in the cookhouse area.

Bear, Jones, and I, along with several rousties and performers, were gathered under the tent lights as nighttime set in. As we watched Bugg and Croak play fetch with Batts, we were shocked to see Zee coming across the lot with two cops no one recognized. I felt a sense of foreboding when I noticed Zee holding several newspapers in his hand.

Instinctively, I knew they were coming after me. Everything within me had been expecting such a moment. Zee was evil. He was a man who wore darkness like a sledgehammer.

"Stop where you are!" Jones signaled as he jumped to his feet and held out his hand. "We're closed! What the hell are you doing bringing cops here, Zee?"

Zee ignored Jones and focused on the cops. "See," he said, pointing to the newspapers, "look at these two photos. Here is the old man in the Ferris wheel article, and there he was when he first escaped with the girl. Look at the Wanted notice. He just changed his looks. Everyone knew him only as Gramps, but when he was dying, I heard his wife call him Reese. That guy in the newspaper photo is the man you've been looking for. Reese Merrill."

It was jarring to hear my real surname said in public, and

even more shocking to realize that they had finally caught up with me.

Croak, who was watching everything, pretended he was talking to Batts and called, "Hey, rube!" Upon hearing the distress call, Bugg and the other carnies took notice and slowly closed in around us.

"That's him all right, without a doubt," the second cop said while comparing the photos. "I'll be damned. That dead carny is the guy we've been looking for all these years."

"I told you it was him. And there's the girl right there."

I was horrified to see Zee pointing in my direction. I grabbed Bear's arm as panic washed over me. Zee had a look of malice on his face, as though he wanted to punish me for seeing through him.

"She's hiding out here, but she's not legal age, and they all know it. That means everyone who is helping her is an accomplice to kidnapping, right? This flyer promises a reward for information regarding the abduction, so I expect to collect." Zee once again pointed in my direction.

"He's full of bull crap. Now get off the lot," Jones ordered the cops. "And take that scumbag with you."

"You don't own this land, sir. You lease it with our permission. And if this gentleman is correct, we need to take the girl with us. You know there are strict laws regarding underage runaways."

"I believe there are also laws against trespassing. Our gates were locked, so you entered illegally." Jones shot Zee an icy stare.

"We don't want any trouble, and nobody is going to hurt her. She's a minor with no guardians, so the children's welfare authorities need to see to it that she has a proper home until she reaches legal age. I'm sure you're aware of state law."

"She has a proper home right here, pal."

"Sir, need I remind you that you are already in danger of losing your license because of the fatal accident that occurred here? If you've been traveling with a minor who is a fugitive, we could have your license revoked throughout the entire state of New York, or worse, especially if you have known all along that she's underage. But there's no need for any of that if you all relax and cooperate."

"Don't let them take me, Bear," I whispered.

"Listen to me," he said under his breath, "there is no way you can hide from them anymore. They intend to take you with them, so you have to get away from here. I'm going to stop them, and when I do, you need to make a run for it."

"I'm not going anywhere without you."

"Yes, you are, Rainy. You must. I will catch up with you. Remember that place you told me about--the place where you used to go with your grandfather and Prim?"

"Jukie's?"

"Shh. Yes. Go there after it closes. It's already dark, but I'll find you."

One cop suddenly stepped forward as if to escort me off the lot. "Miss, please come with us and cooperate. We're just doing our job."

"All right then," I said as I stood up. When Jones made a protective move in my direction, I signaled him to remain where he was.

As the police officer politely waited for me to walk over to him, Zee threw down the newspaper and boldly shoved past him, making a move in my direction.

"Go now, Rainy!" Bear ordered.

"I knew it! She's making a run for it!" Zee yelled.

I was only a few steps ahead of Zee when Bear tackled him and took him to the ground. "Run, Rainy!" Bear yelled just as Croak and Jones jumped into the fracas.

As Bear struggled to restrain Zee, I got an advantage over the two cops before they began chasing me along the fence line.

There were no visible openings in the wire, so I was trapped on the carnival grounds like an animal in a cage with no way to break free. I knew I couldn't bear to live in captivity as a ward of the State, so I kept running. The back exit fence had already been locked for the night, so my only way out would be the same way I had once come in.

"You are in Endicott, Rainy," I told myself, "and you know this area better than they do. Find the rocks."

As I ran along the fence line, my eyes scanned the shadows in search of an outcropping, but nothing was visible in the dark. I thought I had somehow missed the rock formation, so I started to turn back, but the cops were closing in on me. I turned around again and kept running.

I was losing faith when I saw the outline of three large rocks in the field, the same rocks that had always interfered with the efforts of the carnies to secure the fence along the lower half. When I got to the rocks, I reached down to feel the bottom edge of the wire. True to my memory, the chain link slacked near the irregularly shaped rocks, just as it had when Tommy DiGiovanni and I first sneaked into the carnival three years earlier.

I threw myself onto the ground and dug my elbows into the dirt, relieved to know I still could do a belly crawl. As I heard the footsteps grow closer, I thrust myself forward, but the sharp wire dug into my back and slowed me down. Sweat burned my eyes while I reached behind me to unhook my shirt. When it wouldn't give way, I yanked it hard until the fabric ripped. My pursuers were so close that I was sure they would grab me before I could clear the hole in the fence.

Still on my stomach, I was halfway under the fence just as

they caught up with me. When I heard heavy breathing, I made a last-minute desperate attempt to drag myself forward to get beyond the fence to the other side.

"No!" I cried as a hand reached down toward my back. The hand grabbed my shirt, holding me in place as I struggled to get free.

"Rainy," a voice said. When I turned my head to the side, I saw the shoes.

Suddenly, I relaxed my body into the dirt and smiled. I knew those worn leather shoes well. They belonged to Bugg. Just as he had done when I was barely fourteen years old, the big guy was there to save me. Bugg lifted the chain link higher and waited for me to clear the fence before he turned back to confront the cops who had closed in around him.

"I love you, Bugg," I cried.

"Free," he yelled after me as I headed down the wooded hillside along the overgrown pathway to the creek … the path back to my childhood.

39

THE UNTRAVELED ROAD

I made my way across the creek and up Elm Street before reaching Jennings, the street where I once lived. My past suddenly came alive again, just like that scene in "A Christmas Carol" when Ebenezer Scrooge is confronted with The Ghost of Christmas Past.

I felt pangs of sadness and longing as I ran past our garage apartment, which was clearly visible in the light from the street lamp. The metal trellis that I scaled when I sneaked out at night was now tilted to one side, and the old wood structure was badly in need of a coat of paint. The voices of my family called out to me as I paused to listen, memorizing each detail before saying goodbye one last time. "I love you all," I whispered, and then I kept running.

I continued along Jennings Street, stopping for breath only when necessary. Everything was still familiar, yet strange. For a moment, I was disoriented when I passed by the corner of Page Avenue where the neighborhood candy shop used to be. It was no longer there. In its place was a hardware store; and in the display window where there had once been a miniature carousel of candy bars surrounded by cascading mounds of penny candy in riotous colors, now lay a neat pile of steely precision tools under a jarring night light. I felt a rush of indescribable sadness.

Suddenly, it occurred to me that Jukie's may no longer be there either. If Jukie's was gone, how would Bear ever find me again?

My heart was pounding as I raced along Nanticoke Avenue to the block where Jukie's was located. With a great sense of relief, I could see that the building was still there.

After skirting around the building, I ran up the rickety wooden stairs and tried the door. It was locked, and when I peered in the window, there was no beckoning light, no friendly chatter, and no music--only silence. I stood motionless, trying to adjust to another ending. Everything familiar was gone, and in its place was a profound loneliness. When Grandpa died, he took the color and the music with him, and my last bit of hope.

I didn't know where to go from there. Fighting tears, I slumped down onto the top stair and buried my face in my hands. Bear was all I had left, and where could I go so he could find me? I knew I couldn't sit on the stairway for hours or days until he found the place. What if he never found me?

I had two choices--I had to stay out of sight or turn myself over to the children's aid authorities. Although they would place me in a home with strangers, I knew I couldn't sleep on the street, and I couldn't go without food and water. What little hope I had left vanished into the darkness.

As I sat contemplating my next move, I wondered if I could survive within the confines of a foster home. I tried to convince myself that if I could just make it one year under the guardianship of a stranger, then when I turned eighteen, I would be free again. And I would find Bear. But Gramps had sacrificed every-thing to keep that from happening. How could I betray him now by giving up? I had to keep running.

As I stood to leave, I pulled myself up by the newel post. When my hand slipped over the cap, I noticed it was still loose, just as it had been all those years ago when Grandpa and old John Joe and I were the last to leave Jukie's and would lock up before hiding the key beneath the cap.

On a whim, I shoved the cap aside. In the darkness, I care-fully ran my fingers along the top of the post, praying they would find what they were seeking. The key was still there! "Thanks, Gramps," I whispered.

As soon as I opened the door and stepped inside, I noticed that the dance hall appeared to be abandoned. When I tried to switch on the light, there was no electricity, but there was enough moonlight coming in through the window that I spotted the old piano in the corner. Grandpa was still with me.

I carefully lifted the piano lid and ran my fingers along the keys that Grandpa's slim fingers had once touched—the keys he made dance. He had brought the room and the people in it to life, and I could still feel his energy all around me. As I ran my fingertips along the keys, I rediscovered a part of me I had left behind when I lost the Rainy Merrill who had a family and a permanent home.

In that room, I could still hear the music. People were calling out bingo numbers and lottery numbers, and Prim was singing her heart out. Grandpa was tapping those keys while I sat on the bench next to him, as proud as any granddaughter could ever be of her Gramps. The room was full of people, and I was not alone. The worn wood floors reverberated with their footsteps, and the rose-colored walls surrounded me in warmth and bathed me in hope.

After I gently closed the piano lid, I dusted it with my

sleeve as Gramps would have done, and then I curled up in a corner and waited for Bear.

40

TECHNICALITIES

I was asleep on the floor when I heard a tap on the door. It was late morning, and Bear had come for me, just as he promised.

As soon as I unlocked the door, I threw myself into his arms. It's hard to describe the feeling of being saved. Truly saved.

"Shh," he soothed. "No need for tears, Rainy. I'm here now."

He led me over to the piano bench and waited until I pulled myself together. "We are safe for a while. I made sure I wasn't followed, so nobody knows where we are. And here are some sandwiches from Melba."

"She is so kind. I will miss her so much."

"She cried when you left, and Bugg looks lost. You can't imagine how sad they all were to see you go. Croak made me promise to send word from wherever we end up, and he will come join us. I hope you don't mind, but I told him he could. You and me, we're all he has."

"I would love that."

"For someone so diminutive, he's a brave guy, that one,"

Bear laughed. "When I was rolling around on the ground fighting Zee, Croak sat on Zee's face. Then Jones landed a few punches. The best moment was when Batts lifted his leg on that scumbag. It was a glorious counterattack."

"I noticed you have a black eye."

"Yeah. It hurts like the dickens. Zee and I went a few solid rounds, but I kept him going until I knew you were out of sight. Jones took a few shots at him too. I never realized how many people dislike that guy."

"He made my skin crawl."

"He had a warped love-hate thing for you, Rainy. I think he wanted you to desire him even though he was twice your age, but he also wanted to hurt you because you ignored him."

"I always sensed that. When I left, I was terrified he would follow me."

"So was I, so we deterred him until you were out of sight. Then Jones fired him on the spot. Bugg picked him up and threw him out the front gate like a bag of garbage. It was a pleasure to watch."

"What about the cops? Are they looking for me?"

"I'm not sure. Your grandpa was the only person with charges against him, so he has been the focus of their search all these years. However, because they couldn't find him for three years and he was in plain sight, I imagine there's a lot of embarrassment there. I'm worried they may still want to bring you in just so they can be the big heroes and find you a home. You were not quite fourteen when you left, so they consider you a victim, and it's their responsibility to rescue you."

"Rescue me from what? I was with my grandpa!"

"I know that, but the police officers don't know you or anything about your relationship with your grandfather. All they have on their desks is a file with your paperwork and court orders. They don't know or understand the relationship.

And I doubt they care. They go by rules and laws and technicalities. When your father died, according to the laws of the state, you became an orphan."

"An orphan?"

"Yes, just think about it for a moment. You were a minor child who was living with an older man who, according to their records, was no relation to you, and you had no other next of kin. You were and still are collateral damage of technicalities. And to make matters worse, your grandfather took you to a traveling carnival."

"Which turned out to be an unconventional but wonderful life. But I can imagine how that looked to them. We all know the stereotypes of us carnies. Are they going to shut the show down?"

"I don't know."

"That would ruin the lives of so many people. And it would be my fault for putting the carnival in jeopardy."

"No, you can't take that on yourself. If they get closed down, it's because of Zee. We all know he's the one responsible for that fatal accident, so they'll be taking a hard look at that."

"What do you think will happen to Zee?"

"He'll move on. It would be pretty hard to prosecute him for the accident, regardless of what we know to be true. No doubt Jones will make sure that all the other show owners are aware of what a troublemaker and sluggard he is. I doubt if that lowlife will find work in a carnival again, but he never belonged there, anyway."

"What are we going to do now, Bear? I can't go back."

"No, but I can, so I will go back tomorrow, but only to pick up some fake identification cards Jones is having made up for us and to let everyone know you are okay. As soon as I get them, I'll return. I'm staying with you."

"I was a liability for Jones, and I am a liability to you too,

Bear. You are now of legal age and I am still a minor. I think there are laws regarding that."

"There are, so we have to be very careful. Do you know anyone who can help us? Someone we can trust?"

"I haven't had contact with anyone from this area since I was fourteen. Nothing is the same anymore, and I'm sure the people Gramps and I left behind have changed as much as I have."

"What about the people you and your grandfather knew here at Jukie's?"

"There's one special person who loved Gramps. Everyone called him Indian John Joe. I remember where he lives, which is close by, but I'm not sure he's still alive."

"How 'bout if we find out?"

———

When we got to John Joe's house, I was shocked to see Pocahontas, his old Chevy truck with the gigantic steering wheel, resting her tired chassis in the driveway. It was nice to know that some things hadn't changed.

Once again, I felt a pang of longing for those times when I rode in the front seat of the old truck, tucked in between Grandpa and John Joe, blissfully unaware of all the looming threats that awaited me like bogeymen in the dark closet of my future.

We knocked and waited for the old self-described "Lakota renegade" to come to the door. I couldn't believe how much he had aged, but the man behind the eyes was still the same. He looked at me for a beat before a grin slowly lifted his craggy cheeks.

"Rainy! The little girl is gone and now look who is here on

my doorstep. A warrior!" He held the door open and gestured for us to come inside.

"This is Bear, John Joe. It's just the two of us. I am so sorry to tell you, but Grandpa is not with me. He is gone."

"Yes, I saw his photo in the paper and read how he crossed into his ancestral hunting grounds as a hero. I did a dance for his spirit journey. Such a good man. A man of music, and words, and good deeds."

It had only been a few days since Grandpa died, and I wasn't ready to acknowledge the loss. There had been no time to process the fact that he was truly gone. "I'm still in too much pain to talk about Gramps, John Joe. I hope you understand. And right now, we need help. We don't know where to go."

"Uh-huh. I see. You need food and money?"

"I'm sorry to ask you, but yes, we do."

"This is a gift to me. I will always owe your grandfather, and now I can repay him through you. Here, take these." He reached into his pocket and thrust a set of keys in my hand. "You take my truck. It's yours. Here is enough money to get you food until you find work."

"I can't take your truck!"

"Your grandfather holds a place of honor on my journey. Now I will assist you on your journey. You take it. You can sleep in the back of Pocahontas. Get out of town and go to the shore. Try the New Jersey shore. Long Beach Island. There are lots of kids there during the summer, so you will not be noticed. 'Neighbor kids told me about it."

"John Joe, I don't know how I will ever repay you."

"You repay me by growing up as Rainy, granddaughter of Reese Merrill, the man who spoke with music."

"Thank you, sir," Bear said.

John Joe kissed me on the cheek before reaching out to

shake Bear's hand. "You watch over her. Rain means 'plenty and bountiful life.' You must always celebrate her." Just as we turned to leave, John Joe added, "And take care of Pocahontas. When she's sassy and stubborn, just tell her she's beautiful. It works every time."

When I looked at John Joe, I could see the connection between his history and my history. In his eyes, I heard the music and all the conversations, and I saw the images that had led me there at a juncture when my life was turning once again. We stared at each other, locked in a moment beyond time and space. I placed my hand on his cheek, memorizing the details of his beautiful old face. When John Joe leaned into my touch, I knew he understood that through the warmth of his being, I saw my lost childhood and felt the presence of my grandfather.

The realization slowly came over me. That's why I had ended up at John Joe's door. My grandfather had led me there. I slowly removed my hand from his face, withdrawing the strength I needed to say goodbye to them all.

Bear took my hand, and then I walked out the door into my new life knowing there are some things that time and death can never take from me--memories and images that are secure in my heart and soul that nothing and no one can ever destroy.

BOOK IV: RIGHT SIDE UP

41

ROADS HOME

Long Beach Island, New Jersey - 1954

With a few starts and stops, Pocahontas made it safely past the
New York border, where we shouted with relief to know we
would be of less interest to local authorities. We crossed into
New Jersey, but Pocahontas gave up the fight just after we
finally cleared the Manahawkin Bay causeway linking the
mainland to Long Beach Island on Barnegat Bay. (Bear reckoned that the refusal of Pocahontas to engage with anything
Manahawkin-related was likely a tribal rivalry stand-off.)

That night, under a sky of oscillating stars, we cuddled
together in the flatbed of our 1936 Chevy truck tucked beneath
a pile of old blankets. It was a milestone for a girl who had
once hidden behind a fabricated New Jersey past, because this
time, life in New Jersey was real.

Bear and I agreed that our arrival on Long Beach Island in
that classic truck was fortuitous, as that night was a classic by
all standards. One state farther away from the reach of New

York authorities, we felt as though we had escaped to a metaphorical Switzerland.

The next morning, Pocahontas still refused to move onward. We told her she was beautiful, as John Joe had directed, but her battery rejected our pleas to cooperate. As traffic whizzed by, Bear flagged down a Ford Woody with three kids around our age who gave us a jumpstart and told us to follow them back to their flat in an old boarding house near the beach in Ship Bottom.

Their flat was huge, so they allowed us to sleep on their floor until we could earn enough money to afford our own apartment in nearby Surf City, which we managed to do very quickly thanks to John Joe's generous gift.

Once we settled, Pocahontas kept a bored watch from the driveway, disinclined to move more than occasionally when Bear stroked her ego and started her up just to keep her going. On her dash was a feather I had found on the floor when giving her a wash. I recognized it as the feather that John Joe once wore in his hat. It was a treasure I cherished.

Long Beach Island, one of the most beautiful places I had ever been, became our home for a year. Bear and I both waited tables at Tazio's Tomato Pies, a local pizza restaurant offering mouth-watering pizzas and a romantic atmosphere with indoor fountains and striking hand-painted murals of Italy. (Although our hair always smelled like garlic, we loved our nightly visits to Rome, Florence, and Venice as much as we loved the left-over slices of pizza.)

Bear sent word of our location to Croak, who showed up at our door about three months after we arrived. He stayed with us until the last day we were on the island. Of course, everybody loved him because he kept us all laughing at his stories and his antics.

Because I was still a minor and considered a runaway, we

were very circumspect about the details of our past or our life in the carnival. Our new friends thought Bear and I were a couple in our twenties who had taken to the road and had spent a summer working at a carnival where we met Croak. I was still hiding, but the beach and the summer sun filled me with a growing sense of freedom.

The beach and the movies were our two favorite escapes, but even though we had fake ID cards, I was always careful not to call attention to myself. After we saw Brando's new film, "On the Waterfront," which we all agreed was a masterpiece, Croak and Bear immediately added more imitations of Brando to their repertoire as we continued to entertain each other like we did during our carnival days.

Although we enjoyed occasional game nights with friends, it was somewhat lonely without our closely-knit, eccentric community. As Bear once summed it up, Long Beach Island was a very grounded place, but we were accustomed to life on a high wire.

Despite my love for the island, it felt like a temporary stop, but I wasn't sure what I was looking for. My only anchor was Bear. We were still in love, but I sensed he was unsettled as well.

When we spoke of our future, we were uncertain about what our next steps would be. Although we had received an excellent education during our carnival travels, our schooling was not something that employers acknowledged. Bear, Croak, and I all had very specific talents.

Bear, an accomplished writer, continued to sell some of his stories, but the sales did not generate enough money for him to turn writing into a career. I convinced him that one day he should write a novel, which was something he promised to consider. As with most carnies, Bear had a colorful story to tell.

Of course, Bear's other talent was being an emcee.

Whenever he picked up a few gigs at comedy night spots along Long Beach Boulevard, his excitement was contagious.

Croak and I were skilled caregivers, but we couldn't find any agencies that would hire us without resumes and references. We all planned to take the General Education Development exam, but we wanted to wait until we could use legitimate identification cards. In the meantime, we all experienced a sense of inertia.

As my eighteenth birthday approached, I was flush with a sense of relief. Soon I would truly be free and never have to look over my shoulder again. No longer would I have to hide my past or live in fear of ominous strangers whose bureaucratic decisions determined my fate.

The next road to follow was mine to choose. But what did I want? I had been in hiding for so long that I had lost my compass. All I had ever wanted was to go home. But home was no longer there.

———

On the day of my eighteenth birthday, I told Croak and Bear that I just wanted to have a quiet day at our flat. I had long anticipated that my birthday would be a day for cheering, but when the sun rose that day and I finally was able to release the fear I had carried for so many years, I was more contemplative than ecstatic. I needed to find my bearings.

As we sat in the kitchen of our apartment, the late summer sun pouring in through the bay window filled the room with a warm glow. We were sipping Savannah Tranquilizers and listening to the radio when "Sh-Boom, Life Could Be a Dream" by the Chords began to play. Bear insisted that I dance with him to the catchy doo-wop tune, so the three of us frolicked around the kitchen, which snapped me out of my pensive mood.

After we fell back into our chairs to catch our breath, Croak and Bear urged me to open my gifts. I was delighted when Croak presented me with a small pink change purse covered with sequins. A month earlier, I admired it in a shop window when we were walking along the boulevard, so I was very touched that he remembered.

"Unzip it, kiddo," he urged in his odd but endearing voice.

When I opened the purse, I was shocked and thrilled to find birthday notes from Melba, Bugg, Jones, Flip, and several others tucked inside. Notes from Gramps and Prim were conspicuously absent. As I glanced over their messages, I was too emotional to read them aloud, so I tucked them away to read again at a quiet moment when I could sort through my emotions. Only one year had passed since we left the carnival, but our friends seemed far away in a place of long ago.

Bear, who could always read me, squeezed my hand and said, "You are now eighteen and you are free. We know it's a big day for you. Just sit with it awhile, Rainy."

Croak then presented me with a second gift. "What's this?" I asked as I opened the large box he set on the table before me. When I peered inside, I squealed with delight. "Yay! My very own top hat! I love it, Croak!" I donned the hat and posed dramatically for Croak, while Bear snapped photos of us with his new Polaroid camera.

As Croak topped off our spiked tea, a sense of buoyancy slowly lifted my spirits. I don't know if it was the vodka in the tea or just the slow change that was happening inside me, but instead of feeling older, I felt young again--younger than I had felt in years. Like a child, I had the urge to stomp my feet in warm puddles on the sidewalk, catch tadpoles and lightning bugs, and swing on a rope over a meandering creek.

"Let's go jump in the water!" I said. That's what I want to do for my birthday."

"That's exactly what we'll do. But I want you to open my presents first," Bear smiled.

As he handed me the gifts, I grinned at him. They both were wrapped in colorful comic pages from the newspaper and covered with a myriad of bows. I could tell by the shape of the packages that they contained books, which didn't surprise me because Bear knew how much I loved books.

When I opened the first package, I was thrilled to discover it was an album Bear had made that contained photos of all our carny family. Page after page transported me back to the show, a place I swore I could never return to because that's where I lost Gramps and Prim. And yet, I saw only the joy in the photos, not the pain.

"This is perfect!" I gushed as I flipped through the pages, running my fingertips over the faces of Melba, Bugg, Jones, Esther, and all the others. Suddenly, I was struck by a nagging question. I paused and looked up from a smiling image of Flip. "But, wait, I'm confused. You just got your camera, so how in the world did you--"

Bear smiled and waited for my mosquito-like thoughts to light in my brain. "You went back there?"

"Croak and I want one afternoon a few days ago just to get those photos for you, Rainy. And the birthday messages too. We thought you would like them."

"Oh, yes, I love them! Thank you both so much. But where is the show?"

"It's just down the coast in Wildwood, New Jersey, less than two hours from here."

"Wildwood, huh? Oh, how wonderful! I want to hear every detail! How is the business? Has Melba broken any more bones? And how is little Batts?"

"Rainy--"

"Who's taking care of Flip now? And what is Bugg--"

"Rainy! Please slow down. Croak and I will fill you in on everyone and every detail after you open your last gift from me."

"Wonderful! Thank you, Bear." When I opened my second gift from Bear, I was so pleased to see a hard copy of a Thomas Wolfe novel that I had read several times and always bemoaned having to return to the library. The title was, "You Can't Go Home Again."

I clutched it to my chest with deep appreciation, not only of the book but also of how dear Bear was to me. "Thank you so much," I whispered.

"Remember our lively book club discussion when we talked about how Wolfe discovered that we can't go home because time changes everything?"

"Just like it changes us," Croak nodded. "We're no longer the same as we were when we left home."

After sitting for a moment in silence, I finally responded. "That's what I've been trying to do since Gramps and I left Endicott, haven't I? Our departure was so sudden and unexpected that I was never able to let go of the past."

"I think maybe you're right, Rainy."

"Ever since Gramps and I left home, I've been trying to go back there--back to who I was. But I can't ever go back. I think that's what you're telling me, Bear."

"I'm not telling you anything you don't already know, Rainy Merrill."

"'Rainy Merrill.' I like my name. But I had to hide my identity for so long that I thought I had disappeared. I had only half a name, as though I were half a person. But I was always Rainy. And although I can't recapture what was lost, I have gained so much."

"Is that why Wolfe's book has always spoken to you?"

"Yes, even though I didn't realize it then. But I think you knew that long before I did," I grinned.

"Of course. I'm a lot smarter than I look," he grinned.

"Thank God for that!" Croak chimed in.

"You don't say many words, Croak," Bear joked, "but when you do, it's too many."

We sat at the table laughing for a long time. It was a wonderful birthday. I stared at them both, thinking back on how I had met each of them while living such an unorthodox but magical life. However, I had allowed my sense of loss to color those years I traveled with the show, and I always had one foot out the door with no direction. Everything was temporary to me as I tried to get back to where I had started, and in the meantime, I couldn't see who I had become as a result of my unique experiences. But now, my direction was mine to choose.

I looked down at my book and back up again at Bear and Croak. The looks of expectancy on their faces made me break into laughter. "Have you been waiting all year for me to come to this realization?"

"What realization?" Bear prodded.

"Bear, you will never in your life be successful at pulling off that innocent look of yours. But I will say it if you need to hear it--home is not the past. Home is the now."

"And ...?"

With a dramatic flourish, I rose to my feet. "So grab your hats, gentlemen. We're heading for Wildwood. We're going home."

The joy on their faces will always be a snapshot in my memory. Bear and Croak already knew a truth about life that had taken me a long time to accept. I was filled with a joy that far outweighed my sense of longing for what was lost.

I wasn't leaving Gramps and my loved ones behind. With every step forward, I carried them all with me, and I always will. A divergent and exciting road lay ahead. I could hear it calling to me. The best part was that I had Bear and Croak at my side. They knew who they were, and I finally knew who I was too. We were carnies.

The End

ACKNOWLEDGMENTS

Indeed, the completion of an arduous task requires a village. I want to acknowledge my wonderful support team, because without them, this novel would still be brain noise.

With each new book, I create a different kind of village--an imaginary one that features a variety of locations and a group of characters who reside in those locales. When I introduce someone new, I instinctively imbue them with traits, quirks, and attributes of friends and family members whom I adore. (If I make someone a miscreant, that part is fictional ... in most cases.) Throughout each book, I randomly use the names of people I know. That personalization is my way of honoring my supporters who cheer me on through my process.

I am very grateful to my family and friends for accepting my tendency to become an unsociable recluse who doesn't answer the phone or check emails until 2 a.m. True friendship is tested when one party goes MIA, but everyone in my beautiful village continuously passes that test. And even though I drop out of life while writing, the inhabitants of my real and imaginary worlds inspire and fortify me and keep me company.

So whether you live in California, Indiana, Pennsylvania, Colorado, Minnesota, New Jersey, or Florida, or even if you're Joel Bryant, one of my peripatetic friends traversing Europe via train, I want you to know how much I appreciate you. I believe you all know who you are, but if you're not sure, feel free to call me, because I am answering my phone once again.

Thank you to my publisher, Miika Hannila, and the team at Next Chapter for your belief in my work. To the carnies who taught me to see with clearer eyes--your admirable courage, heart, and humor was the inspiration for this story, and I am humbled and grateful. A very special thanks to Skip Cimino for the conversation that began this journey.

And hugs to you, Buddy--always loyal and forgiving of my unkempt appearance and sneaky attempts to shorten your walks.

Until the next one, may you all enjoy the carnival that is Life.

Gwen Banta
Los Angeles 2024

ABOUT THE AUTHOR

 Gwen Banta was born in Binghamton, New York, and educated in Indianapolis, Indiana, where she received B.A. and M.S. degrees from Butler University. A member of Kappa Delta Pi International Honorary Society, she also received a language certification from The Defense Language Institute in Monterey, California.

The author has received numerous awards for her fiction, including Opus Magnum Discovery Award For New Literature-HM, Great Northwest Book Festival, Los Angeles Book Festival, Pacific Rim Book Festival, San Francisco Book Festival, and Great Southeast Book Festival.

Gwen has also written several screenplays. Her screenplay, *Skies A' Fallin'*, is currently under option to an independent producer. Awards for her screenplays include Writer's Project Semi-Finalist, Columbine International Screenwriting Competition Finalist, Ohio Film Festival Semi-Finalist, and People's Pilot Semi-Finalist.

The stage play, *The Fly Strip*, based on *The Remarkable Journey of Weed Clapper* and co-written by Richard Kuhlman, is currently scheduled for publication.

An award-winning actress of stage, screen, and television, Gwen is a member of SAG-AFTRA and Actors' Equity

Association. She is also a card-carrying member of Dog-Lovers Ubiquitous, an organization formed by her dog, Buddy, who is Vice-President of Treats.

———

To learn more about Gwen Banta and discover more Next Chapter authors, visit our website at www.nextchapter.pub.

Beyond the Hole in the Fence
ISBN: 978-4-82419-409-1

Published by
Next Chapter
2-5-6 SANNO
SANNO BRIDGE
143-0023 Ota-Ku, Tokyo
+818035793528

8th May 2024